The Enchanted Whistle

MOLLIE HUNTER

Hob Hazledene is a herd-boy in the Scottish Border country and one day he does a most dangerous thing – he steals cattle from a fairy, or a 'ferlie'. When the ferlie's magic wins his cattle back again, spiteful old Goody Cunningham, the witch, persuades Hob to play his enchanted whistle which makes strange, sweet music and steal the cattle a second time. Finally the ferlie's anger is turned against Hob. Danger and excitement mount as Hob tries to avoid being caught in the ferlie's power – but will he be able to resist the tempting trap that lies waiting for him in the bright ferlie world beneath the three hills?

THE
Enchanted Whistle

MOLLIE HUNTER

Illustrated by Michal Morse

A Magnet Book

First published in Great Britain 1968
by Blackie & Son Limited
under the title *The Ferlie*
Magnet paperback edition published 1985
by Methuen Children's Books Limited
11 New Fetter Lane, London EC4P 4EE
Copyright © 1968 by Mollie Hunter McIlwraith
Printed in Great Britain by
Richard Clay (The Chaucer Press) Ltd
Bungay, Suffolk

ISBN 0 416 51780 3

To 'The Bowmen', with my love.

Contents

The Enchanted Whistle

CHAPTER ONE

The Whistle

There was a herd-boy once by the name of Hob Hazeldene, and he lived on the Scottish side of the border between the lands of England and Scotland. He was small for his age, this Hob, with dark hair and a skin that was nut-brown from spending so much time in the open air. Also, he was very good at making whistles from the wood of the elder-tree, and the story goes that he was a warlock who had learned the art of making whistles from a ferlie.

Now, a warlock is the name they have for a wizard in this Border country, and ferlie is their word for fairy, but that part of the story about Hob is simply not true. It was something quite different that happened between him and the Ferlie, and as for being a warlock – well, this is how it all came about.

Hob, you must understand, was an orphan, without a soul in the wide world to call his own, and from the time he was a baby he had been brought up by an old woman called Goody Cunningham. He never knew who his parents were or what had become of them and neither did anyone else – except maybe old Goody, and if she knew she was not telling, for she had not taken Hob in out of charity. She simply wanted to make money out of him as soon as he was old enough to earn a wage.

This was quite a common thing for old women like her to do in those long-ago days, and Hob thought none the worse of her for it. On the other hand, he owed her no thanks since she gave him little clothing and less food in the years he was with her, and he grew up without hearing her speak a single word of kindness to him. He had good reason to dislike old Goody, in fact, but he was also afraid of her because people said she was a witch, and she had such strange eyes – shiny and black like those of a crow – that he thought this might well be true. Goody, however, was clever at keeping secrets; Hob never discovered the truth of this rumour about her. And so the day came when she put him out to work as a herd-boy to a man called Big Archie Armstrong.

Big Archie had been named for his size. He had a black beard, a furious temper, a horde of tall sons nearly as big as himself, and a red-haired wife called Kate whose temper matched his own. With such a master and mistress Hob had to learn to walk even more warily than he had done with Goody Cunningham, but he liked herding Big Archie's cattle, for he had a way with animals; and cattle-beasts being friendly creatures to those that understand them, his first year as a herd-boy went by without his getting into too much trouble.

Then, one fine summer evening at the end of this time, Goody Cunningham came to collect the wages for his year's work, and that was the beginning of very serious trouble indeed for Hob.

Big Archie was in the stable-yard that evening, grooming his black stallion Jeddart, and Mistress Kate was crossing the yard on her way to the dairy. Hob was helping little Marget the kitchen-maid to carry the pails of milk from the evening's milking into the dairy, and all of them turned to look at Goody Cunningham hobbling into the stable-yard.

She came up to Big Archie with one skinny hand clawing her black shawl tight about her wrinkled face and the other hand outstretched for her money, but Big Archie was in a bad humour at that time and he was not eager to part with money to anyone. He scowled in his black beard when Goody Cunningham demanded Hob's wages, and grumbled at the old woman:

'Ye told me Hob would soon grow with good feeding when I took him off your hands – but look at him now! He is still a wee, shilpit creature, all thin legs and big eyes.'

'Aye, he is still no bigger than little Marget there!' Mistress Kate chimed in.

She pointed to Marget the kitchen-maid, a small and slender girl with straight fair hair and blue eyes which looked very big in her pale thin face. Both she and Hob were bent double over their task of carrying the heavy pails of milk, but Marget being so slightly built, Hob was taking more than his fair share of their weight. When she heard Mistress Kate's scornful voice, however, Marget made a great effort to straighten up under her load so that Hob could stand straight as well.

Goody Cunningham noticed this and she said angrily, 'Hob is half a head taller than the kitchen-lass but she is dragging him down to her own size. She is a lazy one, that Marget! You should take a rod across her back oftener than you do, Mistress Kate.'

'Marget is a good worker,' retorted Mistress Kate. 'It is Hob who is the lazy one that could do with a bigger taste of the rod, and he is not worth the five shillings a year Big Archie agreed to pay you for him.'

Hob whispered to Marget to put down the pail they were carrying, for he was curious to see what would come out of all this. He was also a little fearful, for it struck him that it was not very wise of Big Archie and Mistress Kate to put Goody Cunningham in a bad humour. She was such a spiteful old woman that she never forgave an injury, and if she really *was* a witch as people said, she might take a queer enough revenge on them!

Goody was wailing and lamenting over Mistress Kate's words by this time, bitterly complaining of all it had cost her to feed Hob before he was old enough to earn a wage and declaring that she had not a shilling to bless herself with, and Big Archie's temper fairly exploded at this.

'Nor have I a shilling until I can get some decent cattle-beasts to take to market!' he shouted, and he pointed to the little herd of rough-coated black cattle Hob had driven in from the hill that evening. 'There is all the herd I have left after the ones that were lost in the winter storms and the others that died of colic when they ate the new grass this spring! Is that a herd to make a man rich?'

'And forbye,' Mistress Kate added, 'that Hob Hazeldene has a bottomless pit for a stomach, yet we have fed him on the fat of the land for a whole year. He has already cost us very dear, Goody Cunningham.'

Hob looked at Marget with his mouth a round O of astonishment. It was true he was always hungry, but that was because he was growing fast. As for feeding him on the fat of the land – it was seldom Mistress Kate ever gave him anything better than thin kale and porridge to eat! His brown face flushing red with anger, he began to say something, but Marget put her finger to her lips, warning him not to speak.

'So you will not pay me?' Goody Cunningham demanded.

'Not till I get more cattle,' Big Archie answered, and stood there, stubborn as a mule, glaring at the old woman.

For a moment Hob thought she would scratch his eyes out, so angry she seemed, but then a look of great cunning came over her wrinkled face and she said softly:

'I ken where ye could find a good herd that would be yours for the taking, Big Archie, for they are allowed to roam free at night and only a herd-boy to guard them.'

'D'ye tell me so!' Big Archie exclaimed in great surprise, for in those days cattle-stealing – or 'reiving' as it was called, was a common matter in the Borders and this being so, any man with a good herd took care always to have it shut away safely at night. Big Archie had done plenty of reiving in his time and so he was well aware of this. He considered the matter, thoughtfully stroking at his black beard.

'Tell me where to find this herd, Goody,' he coaxed, 'and you shall have your five shillings for Hob the minute I bring them back here.'

'D'ye swear to that?' Goody Cunningham asked sharply.

'Indeed I do,' Big Archie assured her. 'I swear it by my horse, Jeddart, here!' He gave a slap to the silky hide of the great black stallion as he spoke, and Goody Cunningham nodded, well satisfied, for indeed he could have sworn no more solemn oath. Jeddart was a famous horse, the fleetest, most powerful creature in the Borders, and he was the pride of Big Archie's heart.

'Listen then,' she said, and she fixed Big Archie with her shiny black eyes. 'Here is where you will find the herd.'

Big Archie bent down to listen to her. Mistress Kate turned and shouted, 'Hob! Marget! Go call my sons and tell them they must go with their father to the reiving!'

Hob and Marget darted off to the big square tower of stone that overlooked the stable-yard. This was Big Archie's 'keep' – the place where he kept his own cattle safe from reivers by driving them at night into a huge empty space on the ground floor. Above this floor were the kitchen and living-quarters of the keep with a winding stone staircase leading up to them, and light and quick on their bare feet, Hob and Marget pattered up this staircase.

In the great hall on the first floor of the keep they found Big Archie's sons sitting with their long legs stretched out round the fire-place.

'A-reiving! A-reiving!' Hob shouted, bursting into the hall. 'Big Archie goes a-reiving, sirs!'

'And Mistress Kate says you are all to go with him,' Marget added in her quiet voice.

The Armstrong sons sprang up, shouting with excitement. They ran to fetch spurs and riding-whips, and while they were doing this Hob and Marget rushed back to the stable-yard.

Big Archie already had Jeddart saddled. He gave the stallion's reins to Hob while he buckled on his spurs and his sons came running out to fetch their own mounts. The big black reared over Hob, jerking its head up and down so that he bounced like a ball at the end of the reins, but he was determined not to let Jeddart master him and he hung on to the reins with the grip of a terrier hanging on to a badger.

The sons came clattering out of the stable. Big Archie snatched the reins from Hob and leapt on to Jeddart's back.

With a jab of his spurs that set the big black bounding forward he took the leading place in the troop, and with loud whoops and halloos the men of the Armstrong family galloped off to the reiving.

Hob, Marget, and Mistress Kate were left together in the stable-yard, which seemed very quiet and empty after all this excitement, but some time in the course of it Goody Cunningham must have taken her leave, for now there was no sign of her.

'Bring in the rest of the pails to the dairy, you two,' Mistress Kate commanded. She moved off to the dairy herself, and Hob and Marget hurried after her with the milk-pails. When the last of these had been brought in, Marget got out the churn and the sour milk for the butter-making, and Mistress Kate began pouring the new milk into the big, shallow creaming-pans.

Now, making butter and cream is women's work. Hob was not expected to help with it, and in any case, he meant to try and snatch time that evening to make an elder-wood whistle for himself. However, he knew that Mistress Kate would soon find some work for him to do if he lingered in the dairy, and so as soon as she became intent on the creaming, he began to edge cautiously to the door.

Marget saw him doing this and changed her position at the churn till she was between himself and Mistress Kate, but all unaware that she had done this on purpose to help him, Hob slipped out of the dairy blessing the lucky chance that had allowed him to escape unseen.

Quickly, before Mistress Kate could notice his absence, he set off along the bank of the river that flowed past Big Archie's keep; and all the time he ran along this river-path he was hoping that this time, perhaps, he would be able to make the one whistle he was always trying to make – one that would be as perfectly in tune as a skylark singing!

This was Hob's great ambition, and he had good reason for it, for in the stable-loft where he slept among the straw at night he often dreamed that he heard music of a curious sweetness. He was quite entranced by this music and he longed to be able to play it for himself, yet try as he would to remember it when he woke up, he could never do so.

However, he was quite sure that he *would* somehow be able to play this music, if only he could make a whistle that was perfect in every way. He was so sure of this, in fact, that he spent every spare minute he had in making one whistle after another in the hope that, at last, he would be able to make one perfect enough to recall the strange music of his dreams to him.

There were plenty of elder-trees growing along the river-bank, but Hob passed them all by till he came to one that had new shoots growing as straight as a rule from its base. These were the kind of stems that were just right for whistle-making. He drew his knife and cut one of them, then choosing a hollow in the bank to sit in, he settled down to work.

The first thing he did was to cut a short piece from the length of the stem. This done, he stripped the short piece of its bark, and with the point of his knife he began to remove the soft core of pith from its centre. This was tricky work that took a little time, and Hob had the sense not to hurry over it.

As he sat quietly working away an otter swimming up-stream raised its head to look at him and gave its strange cry, half-bark and half-whistle, before it dived out of sight again. A mavis lighted in the elder-tree beside him, and he watched how its spotted breast throbbed with the pulse of its notes as it

sang. At his feet, the river chuckled and stuttered over the stones in its path. Around him, tall grasses heavy with seed bent whispering to one another, and in a clump of purple clover at his side a fat bumble-bee blundered about humming happily of honey.

Hob listened to all these sounds and stored them up in his mind, and he thought he would put them all into the music he would play on his whistle.

The pith was cleared out of the piece of elder stem at last, and this left him with a hollow tube about nine inches long. He scraped at this tube, inside and out, till it was smooth as bone throughout, and then he made the mouth-piece of his whistle.

To do this, he cut away a piece shaped like a half-oval from one end of the tube. Then, from a piece of hard wood he had in his pocket, he shaped a small wedge which he set into this oval cut. The wedge fitted exactly against its sides, and left only a narrow space open at the mouth-piece end of the whistle.

Just below this mouth-piece, Hob then cut a small, square hole with chisel-shaped edges. At even spaces down the rest of the length of the elder stem he cut another six holes – round ones, this time – and that was the whistle made!

Hob was still not sure, however, that it would blow properly, for whistle-making is a chancy business. If the holes are not spaced the proper distance apart, the notes of the whistle will not be in tune with one another, and it needs a lot of luck to get this spacing exactly right. More than a touch of luck, too, goes into the shaping of the wedge for the mouth-piece, and though he had a lot of experience in making whistles and had shaped this one with all the skill at his command, Hob was still a little afraid that he might not have been lucky enough to get it as perfect as he wanted it to be.

Carefully he set it to his lips and blew, and to his delight the whistle gave out a note as pure and clear as lark-song. He tried a scale next, his small brown fingers flickering rapid and nimble over the holes. Each note of the scale came out so sweetly in tune with all the others that he knew he had, at last, made the perfect whistle. With a great sigh of triumph he leaned back against the bank to play it properly, but just at that moment he realized that he was no longer alone.

Goody Cunningham was standing looking at him from the other bank of the river – and where she had come from was not hard to guess, for there was a thick growth of bushes at the place where she stood. As for how long she had been there, Hob thought uneasily, she might have been watching him all the time he had been working on his whistle for all he could tell!

Quickly he scrambled to his feet, wondering if she meant to go straight to Mistress Kate and tell how idly he had been spending his time. He would get a beating for sure if she did so, he thought fearfully, and Mistress Kate could lay on the rod with a heavy hand!

'Good-evening, Hob,' Goody called across the river to him.

It was a pleasant enough greeting, but Hob knew of old how sly she was and he did not trust the friendly tone she was trying to put into her cracked old voice. He gave her 'good-evening' in reply, and when Goody Cunningham saw that he did not mean to speak about his whistle she called:

'Will ye not play me a tune on that bonny whistle ye've just made?'

Hob had no desire to play to anyone but himself on his new

whistle – and least of all to Goody Cunningham, who had no ear at all for music and no reason for wanting to hear it except that she was as curious as a cat about everything that came her way! Moreover, he realized, with a glance at the sun burning red in the west, he was already late for supper. He would certainly be in trouble if he stayed away any longer, and so he made this an excuse for refusing the old woman.

'It's – it's awful late, Goody,' he said nervously. 'I canna stay any longer, or Mistress Kate will take a rod to me.'

'And well ye'll deserve it!' Goody Cunningham shouted, turning spiteful as always when anyone refused her anything. 'But I'll hear that whistle play again sometime, whether you like it or not – because there must be some sort of enchantment on it to make it sound the way it does. You mark my words, Hob Hazeldene!'

Off she went, muttering to herself; and Hob ran back to the keep, thinking of what she had said. She had no intention of telling on him to Mistress Kate, he decided, or she would have threatened to do so right away while she was still angry with him. What she probably meant to do – now that she had discovered the secret of how he spent his spare time – was to save up her tale-telling for a day when it would come in useful for some sly purpose of her own.

At least, however, that meant he would be safe from Mistress Kate's wrath for the time being. And as for the future, he would just have to hope that Goody might forget her spite at him for having refused to play her a tune. It was not very likely that she would, of course, but he would still take good care not to do anything that might remind her of it, Hob thought, and vowed as he ran that he would never let her see a sight or hear a sound of his whistle ever again.

CHAPTER TWO

The Dream-music

It was late, late that night before Hob had the chance to try out his new whistle. He dared not play it in the stable-loft after he went to bed there, for the stable was too near the keep and Mistress Kate might hear him, and so he waited patiently till every light in the keep was out and it was safe to slip outside again. Back along the river-bank he ran then, and when he judged he was a safe distance from the keep he sat down to play.

He tried to remember his dream-music, but as always, he could not recall a note of it, and greatly disappointed at this he began idly playing the sounds he had listened to on the river-bank that evening. First of all he played the sharp, chittering cry of the otter that had looked at him from the river, then he played the chuckling and stuttering sounds of the river itself. He played the sighing pipe of the wind in the grass, the song of the mavis in the elder-tree, and the heavy humming of the bumble-bee hunting honey in the clover.

As the moon came out from behind the scudding clouds that had hidden it, Hob began to weave all these sounds into an odd, wandering tune of his own invention, and gradually as he played this he began to hear a different kind of music stirring in his mind. He stopped playing and thought about this music.

It was not so much a tune, he thought, as the ghost of a tune, with thin sweet notes that sounded like voices calling faintly to him from somewhere very far away. He sat with his eyes closed, listening and listening to the sweet echoing notes of the little ghost-tune, and his heart began to beat fast with excitement for he realized that this, at last, was his dream-music he was hearing.

Tightly he clutched the whistle in his hand for this, at last, was a perfect whistle he was holding, and now he knew that there was no longer anything between him and his great longing to play the dream-music for himself. He took a deep breath to steady the rapid pounding of his heart, set his whistle to his lips, and began to play.

High and sweet the notes rang out. Soft and clear they rose into the air. In thin, echoing tones they called as they drifted away over the moonlit grass, like little ghosts sighing and searching for a place to rest in. With care and love Hob shaped each one, and with sorrow he heard it die away among the dark shapes of the hills beyond the river.

The sweetness of the sounds they made enchanted him utterly; and so, he thought, maybe Goody Cunningham had been right and the whistle itself was an enchanted one. Maybe, just because he *had* managed to make it perfect, he had captured the magic of music itself in it, and that was the real reason for being able to play this strange and ghostly little tune.

It seemed to Hob then that he would be content to stay there for ever playing on his enchanted whistle. But it was late, after all, and he was just a boy who had done a long and hard day's work. Also, the night was warm and the hollow where he sat was a sheltered place.

His eyelids began to droop. Drowsily he turned his face to the grassy bank of the hollow, meaning to rest it there for only a moment; but before he knew what had happened to him his eyes had shut tight, and he was asleep.

Daylight woke Hob again, and with dismay as the sun touched him he realized he had spent the entire night in the open. With his heart in his mouth at the thought of what Mistress Kate would say to such a prank, he jumped to his feet and ran as fast as he could back to the keep, and luck was with him, for it was still so early that Mistress Kate had not yet stirred out of her bed.

The small door that gave on to the stairway of the keep was unlocked, however, and so he knew that Marget must have been out to draw water from the river for the morning porridge. Hob's stomach was fairly crying out to be filled by this time and the thought of hot porridge drew him on. He ran quickly up to the kitchen and there he found Marget, her long fair hair falling about her face as she bent over the porridge-pot on the fire.

'Ye're early, Hob,' she greeted him. Then she noticed the half-dried river mud on his feet and the grass-streaks clinging to his legs, and with astonishment she asked, 'Where *have* ye been?'

'Out all night playing a whistle I made,' Hob confessed, and added anxiously, 'but ye'll no tell on me, will ye, Marget?'

'I'm no a clype,' she said. 'I willna tell tales on ye, Hob.'

'That's fine,' said Hob, much relieved, and to show his thanks for this he let Marget see the whistle. 'Listen!' he said

27

as she put a bowl of porridge on the table for him, and while the porridge cooled he played a jig so lively that it set Marget's bare toes tapping on the kitchen floor.

'Oh, whatna bonny toy, Hob!' she cried. 'Play some more on it.' But suddenly afraid again, Hob put his whistle away.

'No, no!' he said. 'I darena play more. If Mistress Kate heard me at such idle games she would beat me. She might even burn my bonny whistle!'

'I'll no tell her,' Marget promised again.

She busied herself with the rest of the breakfast while Hob got on with his porridge, and a few minutes later they heard Mistress Kate's heavy tread outside the kitchen door. When she came in, however, they were surprised to see that she looked most unlike her usual commanding self. Her red hair was tousled and her face was all creased with the wrinkles in her pillow. She looked cross and ill-slept and her first words were a sharp question.

'Is there never a sign of Big Archie's return yet?' she demanded.

'No, mistress,' Marget answered timidly. 'There's only Hob and me awake in the whole place.'

Mistress Kate turned to Hob. 'And what brings you out so early, my lad?' she asked suspiciously. 'Ye're hard to rouse out of your bed as a rule!'

Hob bent over his porridge, trying to think of some reply to this, but much to his surprise Mistress Kate did not press the question. Instead, she sat down at the table and gave such a heavy sigh that Marget asked:

'What's wrong, mistress? Are ye no well?'

'I've had a bad night,' Mistress Kate told her wearily. 'I had a dream – such a fearful dream!'

Hob and Marget looked at her and then at one another, wondering what was coming next, and with a little shiver Mistress Kate went on:

'I dreamt I was in a lonely place where no birds sang, and I was feared of the silence of that place. I called for Big Archie to come and take me from it, and in my dream a voice cried, "*Woman, do not call on Big Archie or you will suffer as he must suffer!*" And so I turned to run from the silent place, but there was a river in my path. I crossed the river and got wet to the knees, and when I looked down at myself my gown was all red, for the river I crossed had been a river of blood! I woke up, crying out with fear at this – and then I heard music . . .'

Mistress Kate stopped at this point and bit her lip as if afraid to go on. 'Ye heard music . . .' Marget prompted her.

'Aye,' Mistress Kate whispered, 'music played on a whistle. And queer music it was too – as if the whistle was an enchanted one that could cry like the voices of lost souls. I lay and listened to it, for it went on and on, and no rest did I get for the sound of these lost souls seeking their own rest.'

'Who could have played such music?' Marget wondered.

'If I knew that,' Mistress Kate said angrily, 'I would wring his neck for him!'

Hob glanced quickly at Marget, for it had already crossed his mind that it must have been himself Mistress Kate had heard playing. As soon as Marget saw the look of panic on his face she understood what he was thinking, and immediately she began talking to Mistress Kate again, suggesting it could have been the wind crying over the moors she had heard or maybe the screeching of an owl hunting for mice.

'It wasna the wind, and it wasna a hoolet hunting mice,' Mistress Kate told her crossly. 'My ears are as good as yours, lassie, and I tell ye it was music!'

She rose from her seat and began stirring angrily at the porridge, and while her back was turned Hob rose also and slipped out of the kitchen before her attention could come back to him. Downstairs he ran, to where his cattle were penned in the ground floor of the keep. As quickly as he could he loosed them, and urged them forward over the moorland till he had put a good mile between himself and the keep. This brought him to the sheltered south-facing slope of a hill, and there he sat down to rest, leaving the cattle to graze on the good pasture-land around him.

The effect of the fright he had had was still on him even though he was now far from Mistress Kate's questions, and though he could not resist taking his whistle from his pocket, he dared not play it again. After a while, however, the sound of a lark singing high in the sky began to tempt him. He looked around and realized that he could see for miles from where he sat.

He was too far from the keep for Mistress Kate to hear him now, he argued to himself, and there was not even the danger that Goody Cunningham could approach him unseen again. It would be perfectly safe to play his whistle now. And having thus convinced himself he lay back on the grass and began to play the long, trilling song of the lark.

Gradually he wove a little tune of his own round this, and when he tired of his own tune at last, he began to play his dream-music again. The loud lark above stopped its trilling as the dream-music rang out, and for long moments there was no sound in all the sky's wide arch but the sweet notes of

Hob's whistle. Then suddenly there came a loud cawing from a corbie – a big black carrion crow – circling overhead.

Now corbies are wicked birds that will attack animals when they are sick or helpless, and all herd-boys hate them for this. Also, Hob was furious at this corbie for spoiling his song, and with a shout of 'Drat you, corbie!' he jumped to his feet and threw a stone at it. There is no one yet, however, has ever managed to bring down a cunning bird like a corbie with a stone, and so his aim missed by a mile. Still, it served the purpose of driving the corbie off.

It circled round once or twice, and then it came down to perch on a big rock well out of reach of Hob's aim. There it stayed, in spite of all his shouting and the stones he threw at it, but at least it made no more noise, and after a while he went back to playing his whistle again.

It was still the dream-music he was playing, and gradually as it filled the silence again, he became as entranced as ever by it. Over and over again he played it, just as he had done when he sat on the river-bank in the moonlight, and never noticed that his cattle were all raising their heads as if listening to him.

One by one they came ambling over to where he sat, but still Hob never noticed them. They stood in a circle close round him, their jaws steadily munching and curiosity in their mild eyes, and at last he felt their warm breath on his neck and looked up. At the sight of all their inquisitive faces he gave a laugh that stopped his playing, and jumped to his feet to lead them on to fresh pasture.

'It's a mercy for me ye canna talk,' he said cheerfully, 'or ye would maybe go clyping to Mistress Kate about her bone-idle herd-boy!'

The cattle pushed and jostled one another to get nearer the sound of his voice, and he scratched gently at the rough foreheads they thrust out to him. 'Aye, I ken ye're good beasties,' he told them. '*You* wouldna go telling tales on me to Mistress Kate.'

The corbie perched on the rock rose cawing into the air as he led the cattle forward again, and Hob shook his fist at it. 'Aye, you're a clype if ever I saw one!' he shouted. 'But caw as much as ye like, corbie, ye still canna tell tales on me either!'

The carrion crow flapped heavily away leaving him to lead his cattle on in peace, and he wandered away with them playing a snatch or two of music on his whistle as he walked, until he found another good piece of pasture. The cattle began to graze again, and once more Hob lay down on the grass to play. And this was how he spent the rest of that day – playing as he led the cattle from pasture to pasture, and playing again as they grazed contentedly around him.

He found it strange now to think it had been impossible to remember his dream-music before he made his enchanted whistle, for now it came into his head whenever he wanted to play it – which was often, and never had he felt so content with his lot. In fact, that day was a truly happy one for Hob – and that is not a thing to be said lightly, for there are not many truly happy days in the life of an orphan herd-boy.

'I would not care for anyone in this world,' he said aloud as he rose to take the cattle home that evening, 'so long as I had this little whistle always by me!'

This was not strictly true, of course, for Hob was often lonely, and there were times when he felt he would give anything to have even one person care just a little about him.

However, he had learned long ago that there was not much more sense in wishing for this than there was in crying for the moon, and so he walked his cattle back to Big Archie's keep telling himself that his little whistle was worth more to him than all the friendships in the world.

The sound of a great bustle of shouting and stamping and the lowing of a herd of cattle reached him while he was still some distance from the keep, and when he got close to it he saw the cause of all the noise.

Big Archie and his sons were home from the reiving, and matters seemed to have gone well with them for there was a hundred head of cattle milling about outside the keep. They were good cattle, fat and shiny-skinned, but they were very restless and Big Archie was having a hard job trying to drive them into the keep.

He was riding up and down on Jeddart, cursing loudly and yelling to his sons to head off the big white bull that led the herd. Hob left his own cattle to walk themselves to the byre for milking and hurried forward to help in driving the new herd, and to his amazement he saw that the big white bull had a chain of gleaming silver hung round its neck.

The Armstrong sons closed in on this bull. One of them got a rope round the wide spread of horns on its head, and with a great deal more yelling and shouting they managed to get it into the keep. The rest of the cattle followed with only an occasional whack or shout needed to urge them on, and a few minutes after the white bull had been captured the whole of the new herd was safely locked up in the ground floor of the keep.

Big Archie swung down from Jeddart's back, his bearded face one big grin of pleasure, and this pleased expression

stayed on his face even when he saw Goody Cunningham come hurrying with Mistress Kate towards him.

'Ye're late home, Big Archie,' Mistress Kate greeted him. 'What kept ye?'

'The white bull,' Big Archie told her, jerking his head towards the keep. 'Never did I see such a contrary beast to drive as that one, and the rest of the herd *would* follow him. I would have been home this morning if it hadną been for that.'

'Aye, but they're fine beasts all the same,' Goody Cunningham chimed in. 'I told ye true, sir, did I no?'

'Aye, ye told me true, wifie,' Big Archie agreed jovially. 'There was only a herd-laddie guarding them and he took to his heels when me and my lads charged down on him.'

'D'ye mean to tell me,' Mistress Kate demanded, 'that they cattle werena even locked up for the night?'

'Not them,' Big Archie said, laughing. 'They were wandering free as the moonlight itself last night!'

'Ye're owe me five shilling, Big Archie,' Goody Cunningham reminded him.

'So I am, so I am,' Big Archie agreed, and without any more ado he paid the five shillings over to her.

Goody Cunningham closed her wrinkled fist greedily round the money. 'A bargain is a bargain, Big Archie Armstrong,' she said, and shot a cunning look from her black eyes up at him. 'Remember that, whatever happens!'

'There's nothing can happen to a man with a keep like mine,' Big Archie boasted. 'No matter who comes against me to take the cattle back, they'll never break through these strong walls!'

'Pride comes before a fall!' Goody Cunningham told him. She gave a cackle of laughter and then hobbled off clutching her five shillings and leaving everyone wondering what she had meant by this remark.

'There's something here I dinna like,' Mistress Kate said anxiously. 'Ye came by these cattle too easy, Big Archie.'

'Maybe,' Big Archie snapped. 'But they're mine now and they'll stay mine!'

He turned to Hob and told him, 'Keep our own beasts in the byre tonight, laddie, and let them out when ye rise in the morning. But dinna loose these new beasts till I'm up and about. We'll see about branding them then, before ye take them out to pasture.'

'Aye, maister,' Hob said, and went off to fetch the pails for the evening milking.

He was curious about these new cattle. They looked so sleek beside his own rough-coated beasts, and he had never in his life seen anything so grand as the great white bull. It must have been a rich man Big Archie had reived of his cattle, he thought, for surely only a rich man could afford to hang a silver chain round a bull's neck!

Thinking of these things made him almost forget about his whistle for a while, but when he went off to his bed in the stable-loft that night he remembered it again. He would have liked to have played on it once more before he went to sleep, but he dared not, in case Mistress Kate would hear it again and trace the sound of the music to him. And so, promising himself that he would play on his whistle for a long time the following day, he drifted off to sleep.

There was to be a very different sort of tomorrow, however, from the one Hob thought he would have, and if he had known what it was he would not have slept so easily.

CHAPTER THREE

The Corbie

The next morning Hob was wakened as usual by the sound of Marget's bucket clanking as she went down to the river to draw water for the morning porridge. He lay for a while, unwilling to leave his warm bed of straw, but Marget's voice suddenly shouting his name brought him tumbling quickly down out of the loft.

He ran to the keep and found her there, peering through the slatted door set between the stairway of the keep and the place where the cattle were kept. She swung round to him crying, 'Listen, Hob! Listen!' Hob listened, and from beyond the slatted door he heard, not the lowing of cattle, as he had expected, but a sound like the croaking of frogs.

'It sounds like puddocks croaking,' he said, and puzzled, he peered through the slatted door. There were no cattle beyond it, but there *were* frogs! The floor of the keep was covered with frogs jumping about all over the place, and the walls were echoing with their harsh croaking.

'It *is* puddocks!' he and Marget both said in the same breath. Bewildered, they stared at one another for a moment. 'I'd better fetch Big Archie,' Marget said at last, and she ran off up the stairway of the keep.

Hob stood for a few moments after she had gone, puzzling over what could possibly have become of the cattle that had been locked in the keep, and wondering how in the world all the frogs had got in there.

'Well, puddocks are no earthly use to anyone, that's a certainty,' he said at last. 'I'd better let them out of here.'

With that, he unbolted the slatted door and swung it open. As soon as he did this the frogs came leaping out through it, swarming over his feet in a great rush as they made for the open door of the keep.

Hob stood quite still for fear of crushing any of them, and he was so amused by their antics that the last of them had hopped out of the keep before he realized that the gleam he had caught from one of the little croaking creatures had come from a tiny silver chain hung round its neck.

He rushed outside, and the first thing that caught his eye was a herd of cattle pounding away along the river-bank with a great white bull in the lead. There was no sign at all of the frogs, and he was still standing trying to puzzle the matter out when he heard Big Archie bawling and shouting from a window in the upper part of the keep. He looked up, and high above him he saw Big Archie hanging half out of the window, waving his fists in the air and roaring with rage at the sight of the fleeing cattle.

A minute later he came tumbling down the stairs of the keep, half-dressed and still roaring at the top of his voice. 'I'll bring these cattle back!' he was shouting. 'By thunder, I'll bring them back!' He ran to the stable to fetch Jeddart, not noticing Hob in his rage, and Hob shrank back against the wall of the keep hoping that this luck would hold for him.

Mistress Kate, Marget, and the Armstrong sons all came

running out as Big Archie rode forth on Jeddart's back. 'Wait, wait, Big Archie!' Mistress Kate screamed. 'Ye'll come to grief! These must have been ferlie cattle ye stole!'

Big Archie was too mad with rage, however, to let anything stop him now. 'Out of my way, woman!' he roared, and kicking heels to Jeddart he thundered out of the stable-yard.

Mistress Kate wept and screamed to him to come back, but all to no purpose, and as he galloped off along the river-bank she turned on her sons.

'Go after him, quick, ye stupid gomerils!' she shouted, but the tall sons only shuffled their feet and looked awkwardly away from her.

'If they *are* ferlie cattle – ' one of them began cautiously, but Mistress Kate interrupted him.

'*If! If!*' she shouted. 'There is no "if" about it, I tell you! Did I not dream a terrible dream and hear strange music on the night you reived them? And who else but a ferlie could turn a fine herd of cattle into a lot of dirty wee puddocks!'

'Aye, well,' the son said, 'since that *is* the way of things, are we not as likely to come to grief as our sire if we ride out after him?'

'We are no cowards, ma'am,' another son spoke up, 'but what use is flesh and blood against ferlie magic?'

Mistress Kate looked at them with her mouth open as this idea sank into her mind. 'Lord save us, ye are right,' she whispered. 'The voice in my dream said that Big Archie must suffer, and I would only risk your lives as well as his if I sent you out now!'

She began to weep as she said this, and it was sad to see a big handsome woman like her in such distress. Hob felt quite sorry for her, yet even so, he still dared not confess it was himself she had heard playing in the night. It would not help matters in any case to tell her now, he thought. *Somebody* had changed the cattle into puddocks, and who but a ferlie could have done that? It *must* have been a ferlie Big Archie had robbed.

'Come and have your breakfast, mistress,' Marget said. 'Ye'll do yourself a mischief if ye grieve so, and besides – Jeddart is a fast horse. He will soon catch up with the cattle, and it will no be long then before the maister is back.'

'That's true enough,' Mistress Kate agreed, and drying her eyes, she turned to Hob. 'You stay close to the keep till Big Archie is here again,' she told him. 'He'll want a word with you, my lad, for the way you unbolted the gate and let these cattle loose.'

'But it wasna cattle I loosed, mistress,' Hob protested. 'It was puddocks!'

'Maybe,' she retorted, 'but they werena puddocks by the time they took off again!'

There was no answer to that one, and well Mistress Kate knew that. She swept inside to her breakfast, leaving Hob to wonder how he could persuade Big Archie not to beat him for loosing cattle that were not cattle at all at the time!

He went off to the byre and filled the mangers with hay for his own cattle, and when that was done Mistress Kate set him to cleaning out the dairy. It was noon by the time that work was finished, but still Big Archie had not come back. Hob went into the kitchen for his dinner, and there he found Mistress Kate and her sons debating what steps they should take next.

The argument was still going on by the time Hob had

finished his dinner, and he rose from the table wondering whether anyone would notice if he slipped away to find some quiet place where he could play his whistle. Over to the window he wandered and looked out, considering which would be the best way to go, and while he was standing there he saw a horse coming into view on the path by the river-bank. It was a big creature, black against the sun, and it looked like Jeddart.

'Mistress Kate!' he shouted. 'I think I see Jeddart!'

'Oh, he's back! Thank heaven, my man's back!' Mistress Kate cried.

She made for the door and everybody followed her in a pell-mell rush down the stairs to the stable-yard. Out there, they could hear the horse's hooves thudding as he cantered towards the keep, but for the moment there was a fold in the ground that hid him from their view. Seconds later he topped the rise, and they saw that it was indeed Big Archie's horse.

There was no sign of Big Archie himself, however. Jeddart was riderless.

Mistress Kate gasped. Her sons broke into shouts of dismay, and then silence fell on them all as they waited for Jeddart to arrive in the yard. Nearer and nearer he came, his canter now dropping down into a trot, and the trot slowing finally to a walk. Jeddart was tired. There was sweat gleaming on his sides, and his big head drooped. Also, they could see now, he was not quite riderless. On the saddle on his back there perched a big black carrion crow.

Mistress Kate went white at the sight of it, for as well as being a creature of wicked habits, the corbie is also a bird of ill-omen, whose presence foretells disaster. '*I knew it!*' she whispered, and she and everyone else stood as still as stones while Jeddart walked slowly into the yard.

The corbie stayed perched in the saddle, swaying back and forth and eyeing them with its shiny black gaze. Jeddart came to a halt, head hanging, a few yards from where Mistress Kate stood. With a loud '*Caw!*' the corbie flapped into the air, and began slowly circling upwards.

Mistress Kate went suddenly as red with anger as she had been white with shock. 'Bring it down!' she screamed. 'Fetch a hawk, lads, and fly it at that corbie!'

Her sons rushed to obey her, but even before they started off to the outhouse where the hawks were kept, Hob was racing to the stable, for Hob was in the grip of an idea that he had no time to explain to anyone.

The shiny black gaze of the corbie had reminded him of someone, and that someone was Goody Cunningham. And people said that old Goody was a witch, didn't they? Also, she had spoken very strangely to Big Archie when he had boasted that no one could get the cattle back from him.

'*Pride comes before a fall,*' she had said, and then she had gone off cackling as if she were enjoying some secret joke. And now Big Archie had vanished, and here was a corbie with the same shiny black gaze as herself riding back in triumph on his horse!

With all these thoughts running through his mind, Hob dashed into the stable and threw open the door of the loose-box that held a little brown mare by the name of Jinty. Without even stopping to put a bridle on her he clambered on to her back and galloped out of the stable. Jinty was sure of foot, and fast. Also, she could soar like a bird over hedges, and that was why he had chosen her. Mounted on Jinty, he could travel fast across country – *as the crow flies!* And that was exactly what he meant to do.

As for the hawk, that was part of his plan also – if he could bring it off! That would depend on his whistle, Hob thought, and galloped forward feeling in his pocket to make sure it was still there.

The hawk was already loose, but it had still to gain height on the crow before it could stoop down for its strike. Mistress Kate and her sons were so busy encouraging it with their cries that they had no time to notice Hob galloping away on Jinty, and he kept his eyes on the corbie, leaving the little mare to look after her own footing.

The hawk reached the peak of its upward climb, and hovered before stooping in for the kill. The corbie began to bank and turn to twist out of its path before it could come hurtling down. With a quick tug at Jinty's mane Hob drew her to a halt, set his whistle to his lips, and sharply blew the call that the hawk had been trained to recognize as the order to return to hand.

Big Archie trained his hawks well, but even so, it was not easy to call off a hawk that was stooping in for the kill. Three times Hob had to send the command shrilling out from his whistle before the hawk obeyed, and came gliding down to him. He held out his wrist to it, and it perched there with its jesses – the long leather straps that were used for tethering it to its perch – trailing from its legs.

Quickly then, Hob wrapped these jesses round his wrist and urged Jinty on again. The corbie was flapping on ahead, its speed slackening now that the danger from the hawk was removed. He put Jinty to her best speed and galloped after it.

As the gap between them closed, he loosed the hawk again and flew it at the corbie. Once more it climbed and hovered for the stoop, and once more Hob managed to call it off and bring it back to hand.

The corbie was tiring. Its wing-beats were becoming slower and heavier, and when Hob loosed the hawk for the third time it could not manage even the smallest increase in its speed. He called the hawk in again and with the feeblest of caws the corbie flapped down to perch on a pile of stones. It stayed there, sidling uneasily about, but making no attempt to fly off again while Hob rode Jinty up to it.

He pulled the mare to a halt beside the pile of stones. The hawk on his wrist ruffled its feathers and raised its wings, glaring with fierce yellow eyes and mewing angrily at being called off its prey. The corbie moved its head restlessly, and darted side-long glances from Hob to the angry hawk.

For several moments Hob sat there silently staring back at

the corbie, for the thought of the next step in his plan was suddenly making him feel very foolish. However, having gone so far with it, he could not draw back now. He drew a deep breath and said:

'I dinna think ye are a real corbie, Corbie, and I think ye ken what has happened to Big Archie Armstrong.'

The corbie hopped a little further away from him, making its cawing noise and raising its wings as if to fly off.

'Stay still, Corbie, and listen to me!' Hob commanded.

The corbie balanced itself with flapping wings on the pile of stones and Hob said sharply, 'Ye can fly off now, Corbie – but fly nice and slow, and take me to the place where Big Archie lies. Dinna try to cheat me, though, or to fly fast, or I will put the hawk at ye again. And this time I willna call it off before it kills you!'

With his free hand soothing the hawk's ruffled feathers, he waited for the corbie to move. For a few moments it stayed where it was on the rocks, giving a hop here and a hop there, and every now and then a little shake and flap of its wings.

Hob began to feel very foolish indeed. If this bird really was a corbie and not – as he thought it was – the old witch Goody Cunningham in the shape of a corbie, all he would get for his trouble would be a beating for taking Jinty and another for calling off the hawk.

The corbie was making up its mind to fly. It swayed for a few seconds on the edge of the stones with its wings spread, and then flapped into the air. The hawk tensed itself for flight also, but Hob spoke soothingly to it, tightened the grip of its jesses round his wrist and put Jinty to the trot after the corbie.

It was flying low, at hardly more than a man's height from the ground, and so slowly that he could follow it easily. That was no proof that he had been right in his guess about Goody Cunningham of course, Hob thought, but he still had nothing to lose and maybe everything to gain by keeping it in sight. With his hopes rising higher every second, he followed the line of the corbie's flight.

It was making towards three cone-shaped hills standing close together in a row. They were not far distant, but they were far enough, for the way to them lay over rough ground broken with big patches of heather. Jinty never faltered in her stride, however, and Hob was able to ride on with his eyes fixed on the corbie and the three hills drawing gradually nearer and nearer.

A hundred yards or so from the lower slopes of these hills the heathery ground began to give way to a stretch of rich green pasture-land, and as Hob rode towards the verge of this the corbie suddenly rose higher into the air and began to fly faster.

'Aha! Cheat me, would ye!' Hob shouted, thinking it was trying to escape, and was just about to loose the hawk again when he heard the sound of someone playing on a whistle. The sound seemed to come from the direction of the three hills, and as soon as he heard it Hob forgot all about the corbie, for the music that was being played was his own dream-music.

For a second or two he listened to it, too astonished to move or speak, and then Jinty broke the spell of amazement it had cast on him.

She bucked and reared in a sudden attempt to turn and bolt away. Hob tried to ride her towards the sound of the music, but he had only one hand twisted in her mane and the grip of his knees on her sides to help him manage her. The hawk flapping wildly on his wrist upset his balance still further, and the harder he tried to turn Jinty towards the three hills the more panic-stricken she became.

It was no use, Hob decided. He would have to let Jinty have her head away from the place and then go back by himself to find out who was playing his dream-music. He let the little mare turn and trot away from the pasture-land, and as soon as they were out of ear-shot of the music she calmed down.

Hob brought her to a halt and slid quickly off her back. He slipped one of the jesses off the hawk's leg, and hobbled Jinty with it. The other one he weighted to the ground with a big stone to stop the hawk flying away, and then as fast as he could he ran back to the pasture-land.

The music was still being played, exactly as he had heard it in his dreams and as he had played it himself. The thought of finding out *who* was playing it sent little shivers of excitement up Hob's back, and with loudly-beating heart he hurried over the grass towards it. He kept his eyes on the hills, looking for movement of some kind, and left his feet to look after themselves, and so he was taken completely by surprise when he stumbled over something lying in the grass. He fell, sprawling on all fours, and saw what had tripped him.

It was Big Archie, lying spread-eagled on the grass with his head lolling back and his arms flung out. On one side of his head there was a big gash with dried blood caked on it, and he had the look of a dead man about him.

CHAPTER FOUR

The Ferlie

Now Hob was no braver than any other boy of his own age and the sight of his master lying like this was enough to strike terror into him. However, he was also a sensible boy, and after his first cry of alarm he wasted no time over trying to revive Big Archie.

Scrambling to his feet he ran to a stream that flowed alongside the pasture-land and there he grubbed up a big handful of moss from the bank. He soaked this in the stream, ran back to Big Archie and let the cold stream-water from the moss trickle over his face.

Twice he did this without getting any sign of life from Big Archie, but as a third lot of water touched him he stirred and groaned, and greatly relieved to find his treatment working at last, Hob began bathing carefully at the cut on his head.

The strange music stopped sounding from the three hills while he was doing this, but so intent was Hob on his work that he hardly noticed this. Anxiously he waited for Big Archie to open his eyes, and after a while he did so. He blinked at Hob in a puzzled way then, and struggled to sit up, but Hob pushed him gently down again.

'Ye've had a sore dunt on the head, maister,' he warned. 'Ye'd be wiser to lie still while ye tell me what happened.'

'It was Jeddart,' Big Archie groaned. 'He threw me, and then bolted.'

'Jeddart threw ye!' Hob exclaimed in astonishment. 'We never thought *that* was what had happened when he came back by his lone to the keep!'

'It wasna his fault,' Big Archie said weakly. 'Jeddart's my heart's pride and he wouldna throw me without cause.'

He managed to sit up then, and feeling tenderly at his head he asked, 'How d'ye happen to be here, Hob? How did ye find me?'

'I went searchin' for ye, maister,' Hob told him, 'and as for findin' ye, I just happened to trip over ye lyin' here!'

'Ye're a good lad, Hob,' Big Archie said gratefully, 'a right good lad. I'll no beat ye this time for loosing the cattle.'

Hob sighed with relief at this and then he asked, 'Where did they go, maister? Did ye ever catch up with them?'

'Aye,' Big Archie answered with another groan, 'but I couldna herd them back to the keep on my lone. Drive them as I would they kept following that white bull, and he led them back to this place. That was when Jeddart panicked. There was a queer sort of whistling noise from somewhere over in these three hills there, and when Jeddart heard it he began to prance and rear like a mad thing. That was when he threw me, and the last thing I remember is seeing him shoot off like a streak of black lightning!'

'Ach, well, he's safe back at the keep now, maister,' Hob said, 'and it's time you were there, too.'

'I canna walk that distance,' Big Archie groaned. 'Did ye come mounted, Hob?'

'Aye, on Jinty,' Hob told him, 'but she's feared of this place too, and I had to leave her a wee distance away. Lean on me, maister, and I'll take ye to her.'

He helped Big Archie to his feet, and with more groaning from him at every step they staggered together back to the place where Hob had left Jinty. Big Archie noticed the hawk then, and frowning, he said:

'What's this, Hob? Ye ken fine ye're no allowed to take any of my hawks out.'

Hob had already decided what he would answer if he was asked about the hawk, for he was still not quite sure whether the corbie he had pursued with it really had been Goody Cunningham, and he had no desire to get the old woman into trouble by mistake.

'It wasna me that took the hawk out, maister,' he told Big Archie. 'Mistress Kate flew it at a corbie, and it came down when I whistled on it.'

'Ah, well. There's nae harm done, then,' Big Archie allowed. 'Help me up on Jinty's back, laddie.'

Quickly Hob released the jess that was hobbling the mare and put it back on the hawk's leg. He helped Big Archie to mount, then took the hawk up on his wrist. Big Archie kicked heels into Jinty and with Hob trotting alongside the mare they set off for home.

It was a long and hard journey for Big Archie, for his head was giving him great pain. Also, he was not used to riding without a saddle, and he would have fallen off Jinty more than once if Hob had not been there to help him stay upright.

Their progress was slow, accordingly, and it was dusk by the time they reached the keep. Mistress Kate had set lighted candles in all the windows, and when they arrived she was just on the point of sending her sons out with lanterns to light the path along the river-bank. She could not do enough for Hob when she learned that she owed Big Archie's safe return to him, and with her own hands she served them both with the best supper Hob had ever seen in his life.

There was cockie-leekie soup, made with chicken and fresh leeks, and after that a great juicy slice each of rabbit pie swimming in gravy, and as she set these things out on the table Mistress Kate said happily:

'My, I'm real glad to see ye safe, Big Archie! And as for you, Hob, ye were a good laddie to go off and search for him the way ye did. A good, clever laddie!'

'And brave, too,' added Marget, reaching down a jar of bramble jelly for the fresh batch of girdle scones she had just taken off the fire.

'Aye, braver than any of my own sons,' Mistress Kate agreed. She cast a spiteful look at her sons enviously watching while Big Archie and Hob squared their elbows to the rabbit pie, and said never a word to stop Marget heaping the sweet red jelly on to the scones and pushing the plate towards Hob.

When the last lick of jelly was gone, then, and the last crumb of scone eaten, Hob rose from the table and wished everyone a polite good-night before he went off to his bed in the stable-loft. For once in his life he had been able to eat till he could eat no more and he was well content with the ending of his day, but tired as he was when he settled down in the straw of the loft, he found that sleep was far from him.

The moon was shining through the skylight of the loft, and he lay for a long time looking at its cold, unfriendly eye and thinking about the music he had heard coming from the three hills. Who could have been playing it, he wondered. How could someone else know the music that belonged to *his* dream? And suddenly it struck him that there was nothing to stop him from going back to the place where he had found Big Archie and finding out the answer to these questions.

He would have to go on foot, of course, because he could not risk being discovered taking Jinty again without permission, but so long as he was quiet enough about it, he told himself, no one would see or hear him leave the stable-loft. Then he thought of the mysterious accident that had befallen Big Archie at the three hills and the long, moon-haunted miles he would have to travel to reach them, and his courage failed him.

'I would be feared to go there by my lone self,' he muttered. Turning over in the straw he tried hard to go to sleep and this time he did manage to drop off, but it was only a light doze he fell into, not a real sleep, and he wakened from it again with the idea of finding out about the music as strong as ever in his mind.

The moon was down now. There was only a faint trace of light coming through the skylight, and looking up at it Hob suddenly decided that he *would* go back to the three hills. It would soon be morning, after all. The sun would be up before he reached them, and surely there was no very great harm could come to him in the broad light of day!

With his mind made up to this he wriggled out of the straw and went down the ladder that led to the stable below the loft. His bare feet made no sound on the earthen floor as he padded through the stable, but the horses there knew him and snickered greetings to him as he passed. He hushed them down, quietly unbolted the door, and slipping through the opening he bolted it as quietly again behind him.

Outside it was dark, though not quite so dark as he had expected it to be. There was quite a lot of greyish-yellow light in the sky, and once he was clear of the keep he could see the outlines of such things as bushes quite plainly. All the same, he found, it was an odd and rather frightening business to be abroad at that hour.

The paths he had to follow were in deep shadow in spite of the light in the sky. Every now and then he could hear a sudden strange flurry of movement from the night-creatures in the grass on either side of his way, and the bats that went squeaking past his ear made him jump nervously. Also, things seemed to look bigger by night than they did by day, and they had different shapes in the darkness.

The shape of the hills on the horizon, for instance, made him think of giants lying hunched up in sleep, and he had the feeling that any moment one of these giants might wake up and yawn and stretch out a long stone arm to grab him up. The hair rose on his head at this thought, and when an owl swooped soundless past his face he almost died of fright.

He did not stop, however, for by that time he had as far back to go as he had forward and surely, he thought, it must soon be daylight now! So, with this hope to hold on to, he trotted boldly on, often tripping over heather-stems and stumbling over stones he did not see till it was too late to avoid them, but always heading in the direction of the three hills. And always, of course, looking for that little hint of red in the sky that would tell him of day breaking before he reached them.

It came at last – not red, exactly, but a flush of yellowish-pink light that glowed in the sky like a lamp shining behind drawn curtains. Gradually the pink deepened to the red Hob had expected to see. The yellow shone a brighter gold through the red. The tremble and shimmer of yellow steadied and hardened into a round edge of fierce, bright gold – and there was the sun rising above the hills!

Hob had slowed down to watch all this, and he was so taken up with it that he never realized how near he had come to the pasture where he had found Big Archie, but as the golden edge of the sun rose higher over the horizon he looked ahead and saw that he had not far to go before he reached it. The coming of day had banished most of his fears, just as the sun was banishing all the strange shapes and shadows of the night, and eager to put this last short distance behind him, he broke into a run that soon brought him into sight of the pasture.

Like a green glistening carpet it lay spread out before him in the morning sun, and to his wonder and surprise he saw that the ferlie cattle were grazing there, with the great bull at their head shining white against this shining green. Hob slowed his pace again to take in this scene, and as he did so he saw that there was a herd-boy sitting cross-legged on the grass beside the cattle.

He was dressed in a cloak and a wide-brimmed hat and his back was towards Hob, but from his size and build he judged the stranger to be about the same age as himself. He halted for a moment, thinking of what he should say to him, and while he was standing like this he saw a movement of the thin shoulders under the cloak. The stranger herd-boy raised his hands in front of him, and the next instant Hob heard the first notes of his dream-music rising softly into the air.

Spell-bound, he stood listening for a few moments and then walked forward again. He moved slowly, not because he was afraid any more – there was nothing to be afraid of in a herd-boy like himself, after all – but because he wanted to listen to the music as he went. Accordingly, he took no trouble to soften the sound of his steps, but although the other must have heard his feet swishing through the grass he did not turn round to see who was there, nor did he stop his playing.

Hob came to a halt again a few feet behind the stranger herd-boy and waited patiently for the end of the tune. The white bull raised its head to look at him, and stood like this, as still as a white stone statue of a bull. The silver chain round its strong neck sparkled in the sun, and Hob thought to himself that it was no wonder Big Archie had tried to steal the ferlie herd. That bull alone would be worth a mint of money to any man!

The last note of the dream-music died away. Eagerly he asked, 'Where did you learn to play such music?' and waited, smiling, for an answer to his question.

The herd-boy's head turned slowly round to him, and Hob's smile changed to a gasp when he saw the face that had been hidden by the wide-brimmed hat.

It was not the boy's face the stranger's build had led him to expect. It was the face of an old man – and not just the face of a seventy, or eighty, or even a ninety-year-old man at that! This face was centuries old! It was as brown as the earth and as wrinkled as the river running past Big Archie's keep. The eyes in it were dark as peat-bogs, and cunning flickered in them like fish flickering in the depths of deep brown pools.

With astonishment and not a little fear, Hob stared at it. If he had seen such a face by moonlight, he was thinking, he might have been able to deceive himself that he had imagined it! But this was morning, and the sun was shining brightly. Its light was falling full on every line and wrinkle of the face presented to him, and he had to admit that it was no herd-boy he was seeing. It was – it *must* be, he thought – the Ferlie himself!

Through the whirl of his thoughts he heard the Ferlie reply to the question he had blurted out. 'Where did I learn?' he was saying. 'I learned from myself, of course. The music is *my* music!'

'*Your* music?' Hob repeated stupidly. 'But – but how can that be? I've heard it in a dream.'

'That's not so strange,' the Ferlie told him. 'Sometimes I play in people's dreams.'

As Hob stood thinking over this mysterious remark, the Ferlie fixed him with the gaze of his ancient, cunning eyes. 'You are the boy,' he said, 'that came to find Big Archie.'

'How do *you* ken that?' asked Hob, puzzled.

'I saw you,' the Ferlie told him, and still puzzled, Hob replied, 'But – I didna see you!'

'That's not so strange,' the Ferlie said again. 'I'm only seen when I want to be seen.'

A chill of fear touched Hob as the meaning of this answer dawned on him. He stood silent for a moment, hardly daring to speak again, then calling on all his courage he stammered out, 'Well then – why did ye want me to see you now?'

'So that I could tell you something,' said the Ferlie.

He rose to his feet and Hob backed a step from him. 'Tell me what, Ferlie?' he whispered.

'I wanted to tell you,' said the Ferlie, 'that Big Archie will only fall into more trouble if he tries to steal my herd again.'

Once more he fixed Hob with his eyes and Hob could not look away from that dark glittering stare. '*Anyone* who tries to steal my herd,' the Ferlie said warningly, 'will fall into trouble!'

With that he turned and began to walk away over the grass towards the three hills. He raised his whistle to his lips and played as he went, and led by the white bull, the cattle gathered and followed him.

Hob stood staring after them, for the Ferlie was walking towards the middle one of the three hills and the face of it was steep, with no place that he could see for the cattle to graze. Yet still the Ferlie walked steadily towards it with the cattle closely bunched behind him. Hob's eyes began to water with the strain of watching so intently. He blinked to clear his sight and, in the flash of time it took for that blink of his eyelashes, the Ferlie and his herd vanished!

For a moment, as he stared at the empty hill-side, Hob was tempted to run forward and look closely at the place where they had disappeared, but common-sense warned him not to anger the Ferlie by prying into his secrets. Slowly he turned to walk away, and as he did so he was thinking of all the stories he had heard about ferlies and deciding that they must be true.

They were not mortal, he had been told, and they had the terrible wisdom of those who live for ever. Also, they were revengeful to human people who interfered with them – and surely he had seen all this in the face of the Ferlie who had spoken to him!

He would have to warn Big Archie not to risk going after the cattle again, Hob thought, but no sooner did this cross his mind than he realized it would be dangerous for himself if anyone knew he had met the Ferlie. People would ask him all sorts of questions if that came to light, and sooner or later someone would be sure to find out all about his enchanted whistle and the dream-music that was really the Ferlie's music!

They would not believe him if he said he had made the whistle himself, Hob thought in panic. They would not believe that it was in a dream he had first heard the strange music. Very likely they would say he must be in league with the Ferlie to be able to play his music – and from saying such things about him it would only be a short step to calling him a warlock and bringing him before the Sheriff for practising magic! Then the Sheriff would say, *'Burn this young warlock!'* and that would be the end of Hob Hazeldene, for sure!

For a good part of the way home Hob thought of this, and he was so uneasy about it that he even considered throwing his whistle into the river. It was too dear to him, however, and he could not bring himself to part with it. Also, he was a boy who had learned not to meet trouble half-way, and so he decided at last that it would be time enough to worry once Big Archie was able to ride abroad again – which would not be for another two or three days yet.

In the meantime, he told himself, he would be perfectly safe so long as he was careful not to mention the Ferlie or to let anyone hear him playing the Ferlie's music – and hoped he was right to think so.

CHAPTER FIVE

The Witch

For the next three days, then, there was peace in Big Archie's keep, for Mistress Kate kept her husband in bed and would not let him rise till his head was healed. She continued kindly towards Hob, giving him good food and few scoldings, and so this time passed pleasantly for him.

Each morning of these three days he drove his cattle out from the keep and took them far into the hills, for he was quite determined never to play his whistle again except where he could not possibly be overheard. It was only when he was miles away from the keep that he even dared to draw it from his pocket, but once he had it in his hand even the long days of summer were too short for all the music he wanted to play then!

Anything and everything under the sun he played, from the small melodies he made up himself to the bouncing jig-tunes he had heard at country fairs and the solemn hymn-tunes that were sung in kirk on Sabbath days. But better than anything, he still liked playing the ferlie music.

Sometimes, however, he wondered why this should be so, for now that the first triumph of remembering it was past, he found it such a strange little ghost of a tune that it sent shivers

61

up his back. He would feel suddenly cold then, in spite of the bright summer sunshine, and with this coldness would come a great longing for something he could not name and a feeling of loneliness that was hard to bear. He would stop playing when this happened, wondering why the music should make him feel like this and wishing that his whistle was only an ordinary one. Yet it was only for a moment that this thought lasted, for he was still completely entranced by the ferlie music and there was still as much pleasure as pain for him in the sound of it.

One other thing he noticed about the ferlie music was that his cattle still seemed very curious about it. They paid no attention to the other tunes he played. But as soon as he blew the first note of this particular music they would amble over the grass to stand in a ring round him, and there they would stay with their faces all turned solemnly towards him till the last of its small sad notes had been played.

It was strange, Hob thought, that they had not got used to it by this time. However, the tune was a strange one and cattle, as he well knew, are very inquisitive beasts, and so he did not give more than a passing thought to the matter. At the end of the three days, however, he found that he had to think very seriously indeed about it!

Big Archie rose from his bed then, declaring that he was as fighting-fit as he had ever been, and after that there was no more peace in the keep for anyone.

'I want these cattle back,' he told Mistress Kate, 'and get them back I will, though I have to fight an army for them. They're mine, and I mean to have them.'

'They're no yours at all, ye big gomeril,' she snapped. 'Ye stole them! Ye ken fine ye did.'

'I ken that only a fool would have let his cattle roam free in the moonlight,' Big Archie retorted, 'and a man is entitled to any cattle he can reive from a fool! That's the way things have always been in the Borders, and that's why these cattle are mine now – if I can only find them again.'

'But it wasna a fool ye took them from,' Mistress Kate screamed. 'It was a ferlie! Who else but a ferlie could have changed them into puddocks! And supposing ye do get them back from this ferlie, how can ye ever hope to hold on to them when he can change them like that right under your nose?'

This argument made Big Archie pause for a moment, but he was so set on getting the cattle back that he soon found an answer to it. 'Ferlie cattle will fetch as much money in the market as any other beasts – maybe more,' he said stubbornly. 'And as for the Ferlie's power to change their shape, I'll think of some way to deal with that too, once I can get my hands on them again. I'll show the creature he canna make a fool of Big Archie Armstrong!'

'No, he canna,' Mistress Kate agreed angrily, 'for the Lord made ye a fool when ye were born!'

'Enough!' Big Archie roared. In a red rage the two of them glared at one another, and then off Big Archie strode to gather his sons together to sweep the countryside for the Ferlie's cattle. They were not at all anxious to go with him, of course, but in the face of the rage he was in none of them dared to refuse his orders. With sullen looks and much fearful whispering among themselves they went off with him to the stables and in a very few minutes they were all ready to set off.

Mistress Kate leaned out of the kitchen window, still screaming and shouting at Big Archie as she watched him ride out of the stable-yard, and from where they were working away in the byre Hob and Marget heard the sound of her angry voice. They had heard nothing of the argument between her and Archie, however, and so they had no idea why she was scolding him.

'Listen to the mistress flyting away at Big Archie!' Hob exclaimed. 'I wonder what he's done now?'

'It doesna much matter what *he's* done,' Marget said fearfully. 'It's me she'll take her temper out on when she comes here for the milking!'

Hob had always liked Marget, and she looked so small and frightened when she said this that he wished he could do something to help her, but before he could think of anything Mistress Kate came storming into the byre, anger making her face as red as her hair.

'Was ever a woman so put upon,' she raged as she seized her milking-stool. 'Here am I, left with two useless bairns to help me do all the work, while that stupid gomeril of a husband of mine goes off to risk his life reiving ferlie cattle again!'

'Oh, no!' Hob cried. 'He never has, mistress!' And so dismayed was he at this news that he missed his grip on the pail of milk Marget was handing him and let it all go splashing over the floor of the byre.

'Oh, oh, the waste!' Mistress Kate screamed, jumping to her feet. 'The waste of good milk! I'll teach you carefulness, Hob Hazeldene!' And with that she seized a stick from a pile of hazel-switches lying in a corner and laid it lustily over Hob's shoulders.

Marget gasped and put her hands over her eyes, but Hob bore the beating manfully and even managed a grin at Marget after it for he knew that she, at least, would be safe now that Mistress Kate had got her temper out on him.

'Ye've a hard hand with a stick, mistress,' he said with a rueful shrug of his shoulders when the punishment was finished.

'Aye, well,' she told him, a bit ashamed now of the way she had laid on to him, 'I was maybe a bit hard on ye, Hob, but that man of mine had me sore vexed with his foolishness.'

And then, because she was really fond of Big Archie in her own way, her lip trembled and she looked as close to tears as Marget had done. Marget gave Hob a glance that told him he would be better out of the way now, and said to Mistress Kate:

'Never worry, mistress. Ye got him back safe and sound once before, and ye will again.'

Hob went out of the byre, very glad to leave the work of consoling Mistress Kate to Marget. It was not that he bore her any ill-will for the beating, either. It was the false hope in Marget's words he was glad to leave behind him, for when he thought of the Ferlie's warning he was very much afraid they would never see Big Archie alive again.

Long after Hob was asleep that night, however, Big Archie did come back safe and sound, but although he had gone back to the pasture-land by the three hills and scoured all the rest of the countryside around, he still had not managed to find the cattle.

'I saw neither hide nor hair of the creatures!' he told Mistress Kate angrily. 'But they must be *somewhere* around. A hundred head of fine cattle canna just vanish into thin air!'

'Maybe Goody Cunningham kens where they are,' one of his sons suggested. 'It was her that told ye about them in the first place, after all.'

'That's a thought,' Big Archie said. 'Aye, that's a thought!'

He sat tugging at his black beard as he turned this thought over in his mind, and then he decided, 'I'll go and have a word with the old wifie.'

'She's a sly one, that Goody,' Mistress Kate warned. 'People say she's a witch, Big Archie, so just you watch your step with her.'

Big Archie gave a snort of contempt. 'Me watch my step with an old wifie like her!' he said. 'That'll be the day!' And first thing next morning he saddled up Jeddart and rode to Goody Cunningham's cottage.

She was at home when he arrived and she came to the door to meet him. There was a smile on her face as she looked up at him seated high above her on Jeddart's back, but there was no smile in her shiny black eyes, and for all his bold words Big Archie felt uneasy before their stare.

'Good-day to ye, Goody Cunningham,' he said. 'I suppose ye've heard what happened to they cattle ye told me were mine for the taking?'

'Oh, aye,' she told him calmly. 'But then, ye see, ye should have had more sense than to rob a ferlie!'

'But I didna ken they were ferlie cattle when I took them,' Big Archie protested. 'Why did ye no warn me, wifie?'

Goody Cunningham gave a cackle of laughter. 'I'll tell ye why,' she said spitefully. 'Ye tried to hold back money that rightfully belonged to me, Big Archie, and that was why I sent ye after ferlie cattle. I got my five shillings out of it, and you got what ye deserved – empty hands and a hard dunt on the head!'

'You'll pay for this, ye old witch!' Big Archie roared, falling into a tearing temper as he saw how she had tricked him. He raised his riding-whip to strike at her, but Goody Cunningham

only said calmly, 'I wouldna do that if I was you, Big Archie. It will only bring grief on ye again.'

Her eyes looking up at him were as cold and still as black pond-water, and with an uneasy feeling that her words might come true there and then, Big Archie lowered his whip.

'Ach, well, Goody,' he said uncertainly. 'Maybe ye're right at that. But we're quits now, are we no? You got your money and a laugh at me into the bargain, so we can start afresh now surely, eh?'

'Maybe aye, maybe no,' Goody told him. 'It depends what ye want from me, Big Archie.'

'Tell me where the cattle are now,' Big Archie coaxed. 'I've searched and searched for them and still I canna find them, but *you* must ken where they are, Goody.'

Goody Cunningham shook her grey head. 'I canna say where they are now,' she said, 'any more than ye can yourself.'

'I dinna believe that!' Big Archie roared, but Goody insisted, 'It's true, though. It was only by chance, to begin with, that I saw them on my travels.'

'On your travels?' Big Archie said suspiciously. 'How could an old woman like you travel as far afield as these cattle were when I first found them?'

'Never you mind that,' Goody warned him. 'What the eye doesna see, Big Archie, the heart doesna grieve for – so never you mind how I manage to travel far afield, or it will be the worse for you.'

'I *will* mind,' Big Archie shouted. 'I'll have you up before the Sheriff, Goody Cunningham! I'll have ye burned for a witch!'

Goody Cunningham gave her cackle of laughter again. '*You're* no the one to have *me* up before the Sheriff,' she jeered. 'Ye would only land in jail alongside me, for reiving the cattle. And fine ye ken that!'

Big Archie was beaten then, and he knew it. He would have started to ride away but Goody Cunningham said, 'Wait though, Big Archie! I've another score to pay off, yet!' Big Archie waited, wondering what this wicked old dame had up her sleeve now, and Goody Cunningham said, 'It's true I canna tell ye where to find the cattle, but I can tell ye *how* to find them.'

'What d'ye mean by that, old wife?' Big Archie demanded.

'Hob Hazeldene has a whistle that he plays when he's herding your cattle,' Goody told him, 'and there's something very strange about that whistle and the tune he plays on it; because – however far your cattle may have wandered – Hob has only to play that tune on that whistle, and they come right back to him. And so, Big Archie, I think he could call the ferlie cattle the same way – if you sent him out to find them.'

Big Archie stared at her in amazement at first and then in glee at the idea of getting the cattle back. 'I'll take Hob out with myself and my sons this very day!' he exclaimed. 'If he can whistle them up we'll soon have them herded back to the keep!'

'Ah, but the sight and sound of you and your sons would frighten the ferlie cattle off,' Goody Cunningham said slyly. 'Ye would have to send Hob out on his lone. But he would have no trouble bringing the cattle back to the keep. So long as he kept playing they would follow him.'

The smile began to fade off Big Archie's face as he considered this, for despite his rough nature and his temper he was not really a bad man at heart. He looked doubtfully at the old woman. 'Hob's only a young laddie,' he objected, 'and it would seem to be a dangerous business to go out after these cattle. It doesna seem very fair to send him out on his lone.'

'Please yourself,' Goody told him. 'But ye'll find it easier to come by another herd-boy than to come by a fine herd of cattle!'

With that she stepped back into her house and shut the door smartly in Big Archie's face. 'Ah, ye nasty old besom!' he shouted at the shut door, and turned Jeddart's head for home.

Back to the keep he rode with his conscience still telling him uneasily that it was one thing to give a lazy young rascal like Hob a good beating every now and then – there was no harm in that! – but sending him out single-handed on a dangerous mission was a different matter. Not that it would be any loss to anyone, of course, if anything did happen to Hob – but still, it was not exactly the sort of thing he would like to have on his conscience!

Big Archie, however, was not a man that was used to arguing with his conscience. Moreover, greed for the cattle had a terrible hold on him by this time and so at last he began to argue to himself that Hob was a sharp-witted boy who could take care of himself as well as anyone could. It was foolish to feel any concern about him! So he talked himself out of the doubt he felt over Goody's plan, and decided he *would* send Hob out after the ferlie cattle.

When Hob came back to the keep that evening, then, he found Big Archie waiting for him by the byre door. 'I've been to see Goody Cunningham about the ferlie cattle, Hob,' Big Archie said, and he told Hob the whole of the conversation that had passed between himself and the old woman.

Hob listened in great dismay, for now he was sure beyond

a doubt that he had been right all along about Goody Cunningham. She *was* a witch! She *had* taken the shape of a corbie – and not only on the day she had come riding back in triumph on Jeddart's saddle! *'I'll hear that whistle play again sometime, whether you like it or not!'* That was what she had told him on the evening he had made his whistle. And then, when he drove his cattle out the next day, a corbie had come circling overhead and had refused to be driven away by all the stones he had thrown at it!

It must have been then, he thought, that Goody Cunningham had discovered he could play the ferlie music. She had spied on him in the shape of a corbie that day – just as she had spied on the Ferlie's revenge on Big Archie! And now she was getting her revenge on himself for chasing her with the hawk!

Why else should she have said to Big Archie that she had another score to pay off and then told him about the whistle?

'About this whistle, Hob,' Big Archie was saying to him. 'Is it true the cattle come to you when ye play on it?'

'Aye, they come,' Hob admitted. 'But that doesna mean to say the ferlie cattle would come to me. Besides, maister, I would be feared to try.'

'Ach, there's nothing to be feared of!' Big Archie exclaimed.

'Aye, there is, maister,' Hob persisted, seeing no help for it now but to confess his meeting with the Ferlie. 'The Ferlie that owns them warned me that you would fall into more trouble if ye tried to steal his cattle again. He said that *anyone* that tried to steal them would fall in trouble.'

'He did, did he?' Big Archie remarked disbelievingly. 'And when did *you* see this ferlie, Hob?'

'The same night I brought ye home, maister,' Hob told him unwillingly. 'I – I was curious to have another look at the place where I found ye, and when I went back to it he was there with the cattle.'

Big Archie gave Hob a long look and saw nothing but truth in his face. His doubts faded, and he asked curiously, 'What's this ferlie like, then, Hob?'

'He's about my size, maister,' Hob told him. 'Ye could mistake him for a herd-boy at a distance, but his face is no a herd-boy's face. It's dark, and old, and awful cunning.'

'But he didna harm ye,' Big Archie said.

'No, maister,' Hob agreed, 'but I still think it would be a gey dangerous thing to try and steal his cattle again.'

'Ach, away, laddie!' cried Big Archie, trying to persuade himself as well as Hob. 'I took a tumble off my horse when I went after them, but that's no so terrible a thing to happen, is it!'

'That's no the point,' said Hob. 'It's *why* ye took the tumble that matters.'

As usual then, when he was crossed, Big Archie lost his temper. 'I'll tell ye the point, Hob Hazeldene,' he shouted. 'The point is that I'll beat ye every night for a month if ye willna have a try at whistling up the Ferlie's cattle!'

'For a month!' Hob repeated in dismay.

'Aye,' said Big Archie, warming to his theme, 'and feed ye on hay, forbye – the same as the cattle get!'

This was more of a threat than a promise, of course, since all Big Archie's punishments were dealt out in the heat of a moment's rage and he could never have kept up his rage for a month. Hob did not realize this, however, and he said with a groan:

'I would starve, maister!'

'Very likely ye would,' Big Archie remarked, quite unmoved by the thought, but beginning to calm down again as soon as he saw that he had frightened Hob into obeying him. 'And ye'd be black and blue with the weight of my stick at the same time. So now, will ye do as I say?'

'I've nae choice, have I, maister?' Hob said dolefully.

'Aye, that's so, ye've nae choice,' Big Archie agreed. 'But I'll tell ye what, laddie. Ye can name any reward ye like – within reason, of course, if ye bring me these cattle. That's a fair enough bargain now, eh?'

'If you say so, maister,' Hob said with a sigh.

'I *do* say so!' Big Archie told him cheerfully. He glanced up at the sky, all red with the setting sun, and decided, 'It's too late to go seeking the cattle now, Hob, but ye'll start out at first light tomorrow. D'ye hear me!'

'Aye, maister, I hear,' sighed Hob.

'Ye're a good lad,' Big Archie told him, and went in to his supper looking as pleased as a cat that has just stolen the cream.

Hob went into the byre thinking glumly that now he was between the devil and the deep blue sea. On the one hand there were the beatings Big Archie had promised him, and on the other was the Ferlie with all the tricks he might play on anyone who tried to steal his cattle again. By the time he had had his own supper, however, his mood had changed for the better.

To begin with, it had struck him that it would be very interesting to see if the Ferlie's cattle would come to his whistle the way his own cattle did. Also, he had a great desire for another look at the great white bull that had led the ferlie herd. And lastly, there was the reward Big Archie had promised him.

Lying in his bed of straw in the stable-loft that night, Hob thought about this reward and wondered what he should ask for it. Should it be money? He had never had money to jingle in his pockets – or should it be a pair of boots? He had never owned boots either, and he had often wished for a pair to wear on cold winter days. He could not make up his mind what he should choose, and he fell asleep still wondering.

CHAPTER SIX

The Ferlie Cattle

At first light the next morning Hob was wakened by Marget shaking his shoulder. 'Get up, quick, Hob,' she said. 'Big Archie told me I was to be sure and wake you well before Mistress Kate rises today. He doesna want her to learn too soon what ye're up to, or she might try to stop ye going after the ferlie cattle.'

Hob sat up drowsily. Marget held out a bowl and spoon to him and said, 'Here! I've brought ye some porridge. Sup it up quick – and there's a bannock and some cheese to take with ye.'

She put a napkin with the bannock and cheese in it on the straw beside Hob and watched him while he supped the porridge. After a minute she asked, 'How did Big Archie learn about your whistle, Hob? And who told him ye could call up cattle with it?'

Hob looked over the edge of the bowl at her. She had sat down on the floor of the loft with her hands clasped about her knees. Her head was bent down a little so that her straight fair hair fell like a curtain at either side of her face, and her eyes looking up at him were big and blue and very solemn.

She had kept her promise not to tell on him about the

whistle, Hob thought, looking at this wide, honest gaze. There could surely be no harm now in telling her about Goody Cunningham and the Ferlie – especially since it seemed that Big Archie had already given away some of the story to her!

'It was Goody Cunningham to blame,' he said, and between mouthfuls of porridge he told her about the ferlie music and everything that had happened since he learned to play it. Marget listened patiently to him but she did not get a chance to say anything in reply, for Hob had hardly finished speaking when they heard Big Archie calling hoarsely up the ladder of the loft:

'Hob! Are ye never away yet, Hob!'

Hob and Marget scrambled to their feet. 'Now mind, Marget, ye're no to tell a soul it's ferlie music I can play!' Hob whispered, snatching up his bannock. Then he shouted, 'I'm just off this minute, maister,' and climbed quickly down the ladder.

'Hurry!' Big Archie urged him. 'Mistress Kate's out of her bed and shouting for Marget to dish up the porridge.'

He gave Hob a shove out of the stable door, then he and Marget hurried back to the keep while Hob set off at a run along the river-bank. He kept on running till he was out of sight of the keep, then he slowed down to a walk and looked around him as he went.

It was a beautiful day. The sun was shining brightly, gilding the green of the bracken and silvering the ripples of the river. Birds sang in every bush, and the air smelled sweetly of thyme and moss and yellow cowslips. He might never see such a day again, Hob thought, looking fearfully towards the three hills and wondering what dangers awaited him there.

His pace grew slower and slower, and he began to argue to himself that there was surely no need to go rushing straight off to whistle up the ferlie cattle. He had all day to walk as far as the three hills, after all, and it was still early in the morning. He might as well enjoy a part of the day before he faced up to the trouble it would bring him!

So thinking, he struck off to the left of the river, and found himself in a green and sheltered little valley with a burn running down it. There were wild strawberries growing along the bank of this stream and he picked and ate his fill of these. When he went to the burn to wash the strawberry juice off his hands he saw small brown shapes of trout darting about in one of the pools there, and he amused himself for long enough with making sudden splashes of his hands to catch them.

Tiring of this at last, he spent some time in building a dam of stones across the pool. Then he went hunting for birds' nests, but it was late in the nesting season and all the young ones were flown. Also he was hungry again, and so he sat down to eat his bannock and cheese.

These finished, he lay at full length on his stomach idly picking at strawberries and popping them into his mouth. 'If only I could live like this for ever,' he thought, 'I wouldna call the king my cousin!' The sun was high in the sky by this time, however, and he could not afford to spend even another half-hour in such idling. And so, sighing at the thought that he could put off the evil hour no longer, he scrambled to his feet and faced up at last to the task Big Archie had set him.

One question above all filled his mind as he trudged on towards the pasture-land beside the three hills. Would the Ferlie be there when he arrived? If he was, thought Hob, Big Archie would have to find some other way of getting the cattle for, whatever threats or promises were made to him, he had no intention of courting disaster by coaxing the cattle away from under the Ferlie's very nose!

When he did arrive at the pasture-land, therefore, he was much relieved to find the place deserted; but after a few moments of staring out over the empty green space in front of him his feelings began to change, for there was a strange thing about it that he had been too occupied to notice on his other visits there.

There was no sign of *any* kind of life on the pasture-land! There was not a cricket to be heard chirping in the grass. Not a single bee buzzed over the clumps of purple clover in it. And strangest of all, there was no skylark trilling overhead.

Uneasily Hob glanced from the empty plain to the empty sky. It was the first time in his life he had ever seen a summer afternoon sky without one singing lark hovering in it, and never before had he seen a summer meadow without a golden crawling of bees over its flowers.

There was something eerie about such an utter silence, he thought. It was almost as if the world itself was holding its breath – and yet ... He had the strangest feeling that there was something or someone near him, waiting and watching, and wondering what he was going to do!

Could it be the Ferlie, he wondered. His heart beat hard with panic at the thought, and closing his eyes in sudden fear of what he *might* see, he shouted at the top of his voice:

'Ferlie!'

The sound of his voice struck against the three hills, bouncing and rolling back to him in echoes of 'Ferlie ... Ferlie ... Ferlie ... ,' and behind the echoes he thought he could hear another sound. He listened hard to it, but could not be sure what it was. It might have been voices laughing at him from far off. It might have been a tinkling of small bells. It might only have been his imagination playing tricks on him.

Hob opened his eyes and looked around again. He was beginning to feel very frightened, but he was also frightened of facing Big Archie again, and in spite of the strangeness of the place nothing had happened to him so far.

'I'll have one try at whistling up the Ferlie's cattle,' he decided. 'Just one, and then I'm off home. This is no place to linger in.' And having managed to bring his courage up to this point he drew his whistle from his pocket, and sitting down on the grass he began softly to play the ferlie music.

Gentle and slow the little ghost-tune floated out into the air. It drifted away over the grass and wandered around the three hills behind the meadow. From the hills came back – not one, but three sweet, whispering echoes of its sound, and Hob was so charmed by this effect that he quite forgot his fear of the place. He fixed his eyes on the hills and listened delightedly to the game of hide-and-seek the echoes were playing with the music, and gradually he fell so completely under its spell that everything but the sound of the music itself vanished from his mind.

He forgot about the vast empty sky above him and the long lonely miles that stretched between him and home. He forgot all about Big Archie and Mistress Kate and the corbie that had been Goody Cunningham – forgot even that Big Archie would beat him if he came back without the ferlie cattle. There was only himself and the ferlie music left in the world, and the music had become so much a part of his own mind that it seemed to him it was his own voice – Hob Hazeldene's voice, wandering through the hills, calling softly to the ferlie cattle; calling and echoing, calling in sweet coaxing whispers, calling . . . calling . . .

He was not at all surprised, therefore, when he saw the great white bull appearing from the place where the lower slopes of the hills joined one another. In his mind he said admiringly to it, 'Come then, my hero!' and went on playing. The bull came on towards him, the silver chain round its neck gleaming against the gleaming white of its hide, and behind the bull came the rest of the ferlie cattle.

They gathered round him, watching with mild, inquisitive eyes and snorting as they moved the same way as his own cattle did. He smelled the cattle-smell of them, felt their warm breath, and saw the milk still white on the muzzle of a calf that had been sucking from its mother. Ferlie herd or no, they were real cattle as solid as any beasts he had ever driven himself. He could not for the life of him see how the Ferlie had ever made them otherwise, but he still half-expected that they would vanish or change into frogs again any minute.

Keeping his eye on the white bull Hob rose and backed away from the herd, still playing. The bull followed him and the herd followed the bull, and when he had led them a dozen yards like this he turned and faced in the direction he was going. A glance over his shoulder a few seconds later showed the herd still following but still there were no shouts of alarm or warning – no sign of the Ferlie appearing to stop him taking the herd.

There was time yet for this to happen, however, Hob thought, and he kept casting nervous backward glances all the time he was within sight of the pasture-land. Still nothing took place to stop him leading the herd away, although he was walking slowly so that he could keep playing as he walked.

The herd followed at the pace he set, and it was not till he was well clear of the pasture that something did happen.

He cast a glance at the sky then, thinking that he had better speed his pace up a bit in case he was not home before sunset, for one thing he did not want was to risk being alone after dark with the ferlie herd. With this in mind he took his whistle from his lips and turned to urge the cattle on at a faster pace, but as soon as he stopped playing the white bull stopped walking.

Its head went down. One forefoot began to paw angrily at the ground. It snorted and bellowed loudly, and behind it the rest of the herd began to push and shove among themselves in the distracted way cattle do when they are not sure which way to go.

In another moment, Hob realized, the bull would charge him and the whole herd would break up into the kind of confusion that had made the driving of it so difficult for Big Archie and his sons. Hastily he put his whistle to his lips and started to play the ferlie music again, and with the first notes of it the herd began to quieten down. The white bull stopped pawing the ground. It raised its head and looked at Hob, and when he backed slowly away it began following him again. The rest of the cattle fell into step behind the bull and once more Hob led them forward.

After that he made no more halts and he did not stop playing, for now it was clear to him that the cattle would only follow so long as they had the music to lead them. He would just have to risk not getting home before sunset if he wanted to keep his hold on them, Hob thought, and continued walking at the same slow pace.

Once he had decided to stop worrying about the time, however, he began to enjoy the walk back to the keep. The

westering sun was behind him and it was still warm on his back. Leading the ferlie cattle was no different to leading his own herd, and he had always enjoyed sauntering along playing his whistle with a bunch of friendly beasts padding at his back. So he let one slow mile after another pass contentedly by, and found that he need not have worried at all in the end, for the sun was still red in the west by the time he came into sight of Big Archie's keep.

As he drew nearer to it he saw that he was expected. Big Archie and his sons were gathered outside in the stable-yard, their hands raised to shade their eyes while they looked out along the river-bank. Big Archie waved, and shouted something Hob could not catch, then he and his sons came running forward with ropes and sticks in their hands. They fanned out round the herd and Big Archie shouted:

'Right, Hob! We have them now!' But still Hob kept playing, for he knew that it was not ropes and sticks, but the music, that would take the white bull quietly into the keep.

Still playing he walked into the stable-yard. Mistress Kate was there, her red hair flaming even redder in the long rays of the setting sun, and Marget stood at her side looking very small against Mistress Kate's height.

Marget scurried to one side at the approach of the white bull, but Mistress Kate kept her nerve enough to back away to the door of the keep and open it to let the white bull through, and everything would have gone off smoothly if Big Archie had not come rushing up and swept Hob aside with a roar of:

'I told you we had them now, Hob!'

Hob was sent spinning to one side. The bull stopped, as it had done on the way home, and Big Archie quickly made his rope into a noose to throw round its horns. The bull put its head down and pawed the ground, and Mistress Kate's nerve suddenly gave way before this threat. As Big Archie's noose came spinning through the air she screamed and ran for her life across the stable-yard. The rope fell short, and with a ferocious bellow the bull charged after Mistress Kate.

The rest of the cattle had begun to mill about in panic by this time, however. Mistress Kate managed to dodge through them to the safety of the dairy door, and the white bull was hemmed in by the other cattle. Roaring with anger Big Archie tried again to throw his rope over its horns, and on the outskirts of the herd his sons yelled and waved their sticks in an effort to stop the cattle from breaking into a mad rush away from the keep.

Hob and Marget joined in with this herding, stamping and yelling and waving their arms as they tried to bunch the cattle back towards the door of the keep. Everybody was charging about getting in everybody else's road, when all of a sudden a gust of cold wind swept down on the stable-yard.

It came from nowhere and it only lasted for seconds, but it was so strong that Marget and Hob were nearly blown off their feet by it. Blinded by the storm of dust it raised, they clung together for support, but the whirlwind passed as quickly as it had come. Hob blinked the dust from his eyes and opened them on an extraordinary sight, for in the few seconds of the whirlwind's blast the ferlie cattle had vanished!

In their place was a mass of squeaking, scurrying rats, and Big Archie's sons were milling about among these, lashing out in blind confusion with their sticks at the place where the cattle should have been. Big Archie himself had been in the act of charging forward with his rope spinning round his head when the whirlwind struck. His eldest son had been charging blindly from the opposite side of the yard, and now Hob saw them meet chest to chest in a thunderous crash.

Big Archie's head cracked hard against his son's head, and the two men bounced back from one another. Down they went with their ropes all tangled round them, and as they sprawled howling on the ground the rest of Big Archie's sons stumbled round them and over them, all furiously paying back the blows they had given one another by mistake when the whirlwind blew up.

Marget was screaming with fear of the rats as she ran towards the keep. Mistress Kate had leaped on to a churn at the dairy door, clutching her skirts close about her knees, and she was screaming even louder than Marget. It was all too much for Hob, and he collapsed into a fit of laughter so hearty that it nearly choked him.

'The cattle!' Big Archie bawled feebly, struggling to raise himself on an elbow. 'What happened to the ferlie cattle? Where are they?'

'There they go, maister!' Hob shouted, and he pointed to the rats scurrying out of the stable-yard. Among them was a big white rat with a silver chain round its neck, and between gasps of laughter Hob told Big Archie:

'Ye'll need a different kind of rope if ye still want to catch the white bull, maister. He's gey wee now for the size of the one ye have wrapped round ye there!'

Hob's laughter did not last long, however, for Mistress Kate jumped down from the milk-churn and came towards him with a face of fury on her.

'I'll make ye laugh the other side of your face, Hob Hazeldene,' she said between her teeth. 'Give me that whistle!'

CHAPTER SEVEN

Hob in Danger

Hob shrank back from Mistress Kate. 'What d'ye want with my whistle, mistress?' he asked – though fine he could guess what she wanted!

'I'm going to *burn* it!' Mistress Kate told him grimly. 'I'll make sure ye never whistle up ferlie cattle with it again!'

She made a snatch at the whistle in Hob's hand, but he shouted 'No!' and leaped away from her holding the whistle behind his back.

'Big Archie!' Mistress Kate ordered. 'Make that laddie give up his whistle to me.'

Big Archie got clumsily to his feet and said, 'She's in a right royal rage, Hob. Best give it to her.'

'No, no!' Hob cried desperately. 'It's the best whistle I ever made. I willna give it up!'

'I'll *make* ye give it up!' Mistress Kate shouted. She made another grab at him, but a sudden idea had come flashing into Hob's mind and he dodged back from her again calling out to Big Archie:

'Maister! Ye promised me I could name my own reward for fetching the ferlie cattle. I claim the right to keep the whistle, maister. Let that be my reward!'

Big Archie stood taken aback for a moment at Hob's appeal and then he muttered, 'Aye, that's true. I did make ye a promise.'

He rubbed thoughtfully at the bump on his head while both Hob and Mistress Kate watched him, then suddenly he made up his mind. 'No, Kate,' he said. 'I willna let ye burn Hob's whistle. I gave him my word he could name his own reward, and so he is entitled to keep the whistle if he wants.'

Now it was Mistress Kate's turn to be taken aback, but she recovered quickly and swinging round on Hob she grabbed him by the shoulder. 'It was you that played the queer music I heard the night Big Archie first reived the cattle, was it no?' she demanded.

'Aye,' Hob confessed, seeing no help for it now. 'It was me.'

'I thought so whenever I heard ye whistling in front of that white bull,' Mistress Kate said triumphantly, and turned to Big Archie again.

'Listen to me, Big Archie,' she told him, 'for I have had enough of this dangerous nonsense of reiving ferlie cattle, and I mean to put a stop to it once and for all. If you dare to go after them again, or if you send Hob to whistle them up, I'll have him up in front of the Sheriff for a warlock!'

'But I'm no a warlock! I'm no a warlock!' Hob cried out in terror, and Big Archie roared, 'What are ye saying, woman! Hob's no more a warlock than I am!'

'We'll see what the Sheriff has to say about that!' Mistress Kate retorted. 'It was ferlie music Hob played to lead the cattle back here, for ferlie cattle will only follow ferlie music. And who but a ferlie could have shown him how to make a whistle that would play such music? Who else could he have learned the music itself from, but a ferlie? Eh? *That's* the kind of question the Sheriff will ask. And the answer he'll get from me is that Hob has been in league with the Ferlie all along; that it's an enchanted whistle he has — for it was *that very same music* he was playing on the night you first reived the cattle. I'll soon prove he's a warlock!'

Now those were the very words Hob had dreaded to hear. Despairingly he cried, 'But I made the whistle myself, mistress. I swear I did! And I heard the music in a dream. The Ferlie never taught me to play it!'

'Tell that,' Mistress Kate jeered, 'to the Sheriff!'

She turned to Big Archie again. 'Take your choice,' she told him. 'Either ye give me your solemn oath that you'll leave the ferlie cattle alone for evermore, or I'll have Hob burned for a warlock. It's for you to say what will happen.'

'That's a desperate choice to lay before a man,' Big Archie protested.

'I'm a desperate woman,' Mistress Kate retorted. 'I've no wish to be widowed before my time, and widowed I may be if you keep on courting the Ferlie's anger.'

'I want the cattle,' Big Archie sighed, '— but how can I let the laddie burn! It wouldna be decent to get them at such a price.'

He stood muttering and scuffing his feet for a few moments, while everyone watched and waited for him to make up his mind. As for Hob, he was hardly able to breathe for terror by this time, but to his huge relief at last Big Archie said:

'Ach, ye have me beat, Kate. Ye ken fine it would be on my conscience if Hob was burnt for a warlock. I promise to leave the ferlie cattle alone for evermore.'

'And you'll swear that by your horse Jeddart?' Mistress Kate asked.

'Aye,' he agreed sourly. 'Ye leave me nae choice,' – and that should have been the end of the affair, but it was not long before Hob found that this was far from being the case.

To begin with, it seemed that Mistress Kate more than half-believed her own nonsense about his being a warlock! She was unwilling to have him near her or to let him sit at her kitchen table, and this meant that Hob had to scrape and hunt for food as best he could.

He was not too badly off in this, however, for he soon discovered that she was very careless about locking up in the dairy and the larder, and he took as much advantage of this as he could. It was not hunger that was the worst part of this state of affairs, therefore, it was the feeling that he was so unwelcome in Big Archie's keep.

Big Archie himself was quite content for him to stay, and even made clumsy attempts to show he was sorry for the trouble he had brought on Hob, but Mistress Kate made no secret of her desire to be rid of him. Her sons followed the lead she set, chasing Hob away whenever he showed himself near them, and he began to feel very miserable indeed.

It had been bad enough before, he thought, when no one seemed to care one way or another about him, but knowing that people actually wanted rid of him was an even worse feeling. He stood it as best he could for a couple of days, and then he ventured to ask Mistress Kate:

'How can ye believe I'm in league with the Ferlie, mistress, after me finding Big Archie on the day Jeddart threw him?'

'And how did ye ken where to go and look for him that day?' she demanded.

Hob thought of telling her how he had followed Goody Cunningham in her shape as a corbie, but he was afraid to do so. Mistress Kate would only suspect him the more, he decided, if she knew he had had dealings with a witch, and so he kept silent.

'Aha!' Mistress Kate cried, taking his silence as proof of guilt. 'So I was right! It *was* the Ferlie that told ye where to find Big Archie!'

'I brought him safe back to you,' Hob reminded her.

'Ye brought him back wounded and bleeding,' Mistress Kate said angrily, 'and the more fool me for thinking kindly of you at the time! What's more, Hob Hazeldene, the matter is not finished yet, for mark my words, the Ferlie's anger will be well and truly roused by the way you whistled up his cattle. And if he takes revenge on Big Archie for *that*, I will take my revenge on *you*!'

She stalked away leaving Hob wondering what on earth he should do now, for it was clear to him that Mistress Kate would carry out her threat to accuse him of being a warlock if any misfortune should befall Big Archie. He thought about this for a while and then a bold idea came to him.

He could seek out the Ferlie again, he thought, and tell him that Big Archie had promised to leave his cattle alone for evermore. That would surely calm the Ferlie's anger! Then he would be able to tell Mistress Kate that Big Archie was safe from any chance of harm, and that would surely soothe her spite at him.

He wondered what Marget would think of this idea, for she was the only one who knew all the ins and outs of his story, and so he took the first chance he had of telling her about it. Marget listened as patiently as usual to what he had to say, and then she told him:

'It's about the only thing ye can do now, Hob. But go

tonight, if ye can. It would be dangerous to put it off till tomorrow night, for tomorrow is Saint John's eve, and that is the time when the power of the ferlies is at its strongest.'

'I will go tonight, then,' Hob decided, and so late that night he slipped away out of the stable-loft and set off for the three hills. He had his whistle in his pocket, and if the Ferlie was not at the pasture-land when he arrived there he meant to play the ferlie music to tempt him to show himself. The moon was high. The night was a black and silver chequer-board of dark shadows and bright moonlight, and he had travelled the path so often now that he knew every hazard of it. He made good time, and in due course reached the pasture by the three hills.

As soon as he came into sight of it he realized that there would be no need to tempt the Ferlie into the open. His cattle were grazing the pasture, and he was seated beside them with his cloak wrapped round him and his broad-brimmed hat pulled forward over his face.

Hob came slowly up to him, turning over in his mind what he had to say. The Ferlie watched him, not moving or speaking till he was within a few yards and then he said:

'Good-evening to you, young sir.'

His voice was friendly, and Hob took heart from it. He came close to the Ferlie and said boldly, 'I came to tell you that your cattle are safe from Big Archie now, Ferlie. He has promised Mistress Kate never to try to steal them again, and she has a threat to hold over him that will make him keep that promise.'

The Ferlie did not answer this directly. Instead he said, 'Sit down here by me for a minute, for I think we have much to talk about.'

91

Hob sat down cross-legged on the grass beside him, quite pleased to find himself being so kindly welcomed, and still speaking in the same friendly voice the Ferlie went on:

'You never told me your name the first time we spoke here.'

'You never asked me for it, Ferlie,' Hob replied, 'but if ye would like to hear it now, it is Hob – Hob Hazeldene.'

'Ah, but Hob is only a nickname, is it no?' the Ferlie asked. 'A nickname that ye got because you are small and dark – like me!'

He leaned forward, smiling, as he said this, and Hob shrank back from him with a little shiver at the thought that his size and colouring did indeed give him a passing resemblance to this strange creature.

'I'm no sure how I came to have Hob for a nickname,' he confessed, 'but maybe that *was* the reason.'

'Tell me your real name, then,' the Ferlie said coaxingly, '– your given name that was spoken when they took you into

the kirk to be christened and the holy water sprinkled on you.'

Hob searched around in his memory for his real name. It was so long since anyone had called him by it that he had to think hard, but after a few moments he remembered Goody Cunningham telling him once that he had been christened on Saint Andrew's day and given the name Andrew because of that.

'Now I remember, Ferlie,' he said. 'My given name is Andrew.'

No sooner were the words out of his mouth than all the friendliness vanished from the Ferlie's manner. With a shout of '*Now I have you!*' his hand came shooting out to grab Hob by the wrist, and on the instant, Hob remembered that to tell a ferlie your true name puts you in his power.

There was still a chance of escape left for him, however, and seizing quickly on it he snatched his arm out of the Ferlie's

grasp. 'Oh, no, Ferlie!' he cried, 'ye havena got me yet, for Andrew is a saint's name, and there is no ferlie can take the name of a saint into his power!'

The Ferlie howled with rage at the way Hob had slipped out of his trap. He jumped to his feet and Hob scrambled up along with him, feeling puzzled as well as frightened by the turn events were taking.

'Why did ye try to trap *me*, Ferlie?' he demanded. 'I never wanted to steal your cattle. It was Big Archie sent me to whistle them up and he promised to beat me every night for a month if I refused to do what he said.'

'I'm no concerned about Big Archie!' the Ferlie shouted. 'He's a blundering fool and I can get my cattle back from him with the greatest of ease – however often he tries to steal them! It's you who are my real enemy, Hob Hazeldene!'

'Me!' Hob cried, astonished. 'I never wished ye harm, Ferlie!'

'Yet ye have it in your power to do me harm,' the Ferlie told him angrily. 'You can play the music that will draw my cattle to you any time ye choose, and if they hear you play that music long enough and often enough they will never answer to *my* call again!'

'But I dinna want to steal your cattle,' Hob repeated.

'Aye, ye say that now,' the Ferlie retorted, 'but there may come a day when ye will think different. My cattle will no be safe from you then, and so it is now or never I must deal with you, Hob Hazeldene.'

'Ah, but I'm on my guard now, Ferlie,' Hob told him. 'Ye'll no get another chance to trick me into your power.'

The Ferlie was silent for a moment and then he asked, 'Ye're no happy in Big Archie's keep, are ye, Hob?'

94

'No,' Hob admitted. 'It can be gey hard for me there at times.'

'Ye would be happy in the ferlie world,' the Ferlie told him. 'If ye could but see it for yourself, Hob, ye would enter it willingly. There would be no need to try to trick you into it.'

'Maybe,' Hob said, 'but your world is no for the likes of me, for you are ferlie and I am mortal.'

'Aye,' the Ferlie said softly, 'but there are some mortals with minds that are open to the things of the ferlie world, Hob, and you are one of them – otherwise you would never have been able to remember my music, or to play it.'

He drew a step closer, his dark eyes glittering in the moon-silvered darkness of his face. 'Come with me to the ferlie world, Hob,' he coaxed. 'Come with me now!'

There was a terrible persuasion in his voice and Hob felt his breath coming thick and fast in his throat with the strange feelings it roused in him, but he hung on to common sense and answered firmly:

'No, Ferlie. Ye are just trying another way to trick me into your power, and I am going home now.'

He turned to go but the Ferlie cried, 'Wait, Hob, wait!'

Unwillingly Hob waited to hear what more he had to say and the Ferlie went on coaxingly, 'Come back here tomorrow night, Hob, will ye? Ye will see something then that may make ye change your mind!'

'What will I see, Ferlie?' Hob asked cautiously, remembering his conversation with Marget and the warning she had given him about Saint John's eve.

'Ye will see the ferlie company ride forth in all their splendour,' the Ferlie told him, 'for tomorrow is midsummer's eve – the night of their highest feasting.'

'That's no the name I've heard given to tomorrow night, Ferlie,' Hob told him, frowning. 'I was told it was called Saint John's eve.'

To his astonishment then the Ferlie's face twisted with sudden pain and anger, and with a wild howl of '*That is a Christian name!*' he vanished instantly from Hob's sight. The sound of his howling cry echoed mournfully back from the three hills, and in terror Hob fled from it, not looking back or stopping for a moment until he reached the safety of the stable-loft again.

CHAPTER EIGHT

Midsummer's Eve

The next morning when Marget came down to the river to fill her bucket, Hob was waiting to tell her about his latest meeting with the Ferlie. He did not get the chance to finish the story properly, however, for he had just told the bit where the Ferlie had asked him to come back to the pasture-land that night when they heard Mistress Kate shouting to Marget to hurry up.

'I'll hear the end of it later, Hob,' Marget assured him hastily, and hurried back to the keep with her bucket.

Hob went to loose his cattle to drive them out to pasture, thinking that there was really nothing more to tell, for he had quite made up his mind never to go near the three hills again. The Ferlie would never get another chance to trap him, he decided, and all that remained for him to do now was to wait till he could catch Mistress Kate in a good mood and let her know that Big Archie, at least, had nothing to fear from the Ferlie's anger.

Once that was done, the affair of the ferlie cattle really would be over at last, and everything would be as it was before Goody Cunningham started all the trouble. At least he hoped so, and he drove his cattle out that morning wishing for the next twenty-four hours to pass as quickly as possible. He was tired, not having had much sleep the previous night, and what between that and the sun beating down on him there came a point that day when he fell fast asleep on the grass beside his cattle.

He woke late in the afternoon to find a shadow falling over him, and looking up he saw Goody Cunningham watching him. 'Ye're tired, Hob,' she remarked, sitting down beside him. 'Ye must have been late out of your bed last night.'

Hob sat up but he made no answer to this, and with a little laugh Goody said, 'Has the cat got your tongue, Hob?'

Still Hob did not reply, because he was afraid of giving away too much to her, and Goody jeered at him, 'Stay as dumb as ye like, Hob. It makes no difference to me. I have my own ways of finding out things, and so I ken ye met the Ferlie last night and I ken what he said to you.'

She looked slyly at him and asked, 'D'ye mean to go back tonight to see the ferlie host ride forth, Hob?'

Hob shook his head. 'No,' he said. 'The Ferlie tried twice to trap me last night, and I am not going to give him another chance to try.'

'Hob, Hob!' Goody sighed. 'Ye dinna ken what ye're missing, laddie. The ferlies have a grand world – a finer place than you could ever hope to have on this earth. Take my advice, laddie, and go back to see the Ferlie tonight.'

'If you think it so fine,' Hob retorted, 'why do *you* not go there? *You* ken where to find the Ferlie!'

'The ferlies only take whom they want into their own world,' Goody Cunningham told him, 'and they have never wanted me.'

'But why d'ye want *me* to go there?' Hob persisted. 'Ye've never thought of my happiness before.'

Goody Cunningham made no answer to this. She sat silent for quite a while and then she said, 'I am old and mortal, Hob. Soon, I will die. In the ferlie world they are all young, and they never die.'

She looked mournfully at Hob with her shiny black eyes suddenly dim with tears. 'Help me, Hob!' she pleaded. 'I'm old – old and done, but I dinna want to die, and if you were there in the ferlies' world you could speak up for old Goody to be one of them too!'

It was a curious thing to see her sitting there with the tears brimming up in her eyes, yet not falling from them – for witches, of course, cannot weep. Yet it was sad, too, for she looked very lonely and old and frightened of dying. Hob felt so sorry for her that he forgave her the spiteful way she had behaved over his whistle, but still he was determined not to let her persuade him.

'I canna help ye, Goody,' he said, and stuck to this in spite of all her pleading.

Goody Cunningham did not give up the struggle, however. 'Ye'll not sleep, tonight, Hob,' she said. 'I warn ye of that, for I will put a spell on you that will stop you from sleeping. And as ye lie awake ye will maybe hear the sound of the ferlies riding abroad, and after that...' She left the sentence unfinished, and walked away from him with a look of sly triumph on her face.

'I will do what I wish to do and not what your spells say I must,' Hob called after her. But that night, in spite of these brave words, he found that he could not sleep after all.

He was hungry, even though he had managed to get some cheese and milk from the dairy for his supper, and of course, it might well have been his hunger and not Goody's spell that was keeping him awake. On top of this he was feeling lonely, because Mistress Kate had kept Marget so busy that he had not been able to speak to her again. He had not exchanged a word with a soul since that morning, in fact, apart from his conversation with Goody Cunningham, and this loneliness was making him restless also.

For a long time he lay tossing and turning in the straw, then suddenly he heard something that made him sit upright. It was the sound of hunting horns he heard, blowing distant and sweet in the stillness of the summer night. The good resolutions he had made weakened at their sound, and when the horns blew again he scrambled out of the straw and reached up to open the skylight of his loft.

'Just one look,' he told himself. 'One look will do no

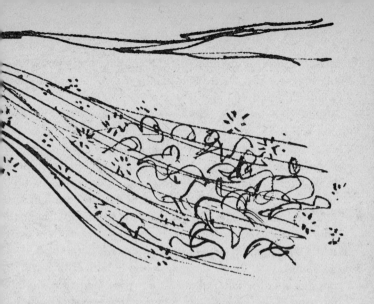

harm!' And with his head poking out through the skylight he surveyed the moorland around the keep.

The moon was up and he had a good view from the stable roof. The horns blew again, louder now that he could hear them in the open, and also it seemed to him that the sound was drawing closer. Something white fluttered suddenly on the crest of a ridge to his left. He heard laughter and a tinkling of small bells sounding faintly through the sweet notes of the horns. From the white flutter on the ridge came a gleam and a flash of silver, and suddenly he saw them – a whole host of ferlie riders cresting the ridge and sweeping down towards the keep.

Their horses were tall and slender-legged and white – white as the moon, and harnessed with silver. Little silver bells were braided into their long manes, and the horns the ferlie hunts-men raised to their lips were of silver also. There were both men and women riders in the company, the men with long cloaks that streamed out behind them, and the women in silken gowns that flowed and rippled like river-water in the wind of their passing.

Down the ridge they came and swept past Big Archie's keep in a soft babble of laughter and tinkling bells and hunting-calls, for the hooves of the white horses as they galloped made never a sound. At the river they wheeled to sweep along its bank, and like some pale joyous vision being swallowed up again in the darkness of sleep, they vanished into the night.

The last of Hob's resolve not to go out that night vanished with them, and he slipped down from his place at the window with his heart on fire with longing to see more of this wonderful company. Without stopping to argue with himself why this should be, he tumbled rapidly down the ladder leading to the stable. There he fetched Jinty from her stall, led her quickly outside and swung himself on to her back. Then, with his fingers twisted in her mane, he urged her to the path along the river-bank and galloped off in pursuit of the ferlie host.

There was still no thought in his mind, while he did this, of the dangers he might be courting. Not even a memory of the cunning in the Ferlie's ancient face came to warn him, but he would not have cared if it had. He had only one thought in his mind, and that was to catch one last glimpse of the ferlie riders before they vanished back into their own world.

There was no doubt about the direction they were taking. They were headed towards the three hills, and Hob reckoned he was not far behind them for he could still hear the sound of the horn-calls quite clearly. He kept Jinty at the gallop, crouching low on her neck and coaxing her to her very best speed, and the little mare answered gallantly to his urging.

Mile after mile flew past under her hooves. The horn-calls

began to sound more loudly in Hob's ears and he was beginning to think he would be able to catch up with the ferlie host when, just a short distance from the pasture-land, disaster struck him and Jinty.

The mare stumbled in her stride and Hob was almost thrown. He managed to keep his seat and Jinty went on again, but she had only taken two or three strides when Hob realized she was limping. He pulled her to a halt and slid down from her back.

If she was in pain, he decided, he could not possibly try to make her pick up her former pace, and he began looking for the cause of her limp.

He found it quickly. Jinty herself had not been hurt by her stumble, but she had cast the shoe of her near-side hoof, and it was this that was causing the unevenness in her stride. Hob knew perfectly well that he would be in trouble for taking Jinty out without leave, but if he brought her back in such a state he would be in a great deal more trouble, and so he searched around in the grass until he had found the missing shoe.

Slipping it into his pocket then, he considered what he should do. There was no longer any sound of the ferlie host, and so it seemed that he had probably lost them for good. However, he thought, there was a chance that they might be gathered at the pasture-land for some purpose, and so he mounted Jinty again and rode slowly on till he came in sight of it.

There was no one there. The pasture-land lay bare and deserted under the moon, but there was a faint glow of light coming from the middle one of the three hills, and Hob's disappointment changed quickly to curiosity when he saw this.

For a few moments he sat staring at it and wondering what it could be, and then he urged Jinty towards it.

Jinty, however, was no more willing to set foot on the pasture-land than she had been before, and so trusting to luck that she would stay where he left her, Hob slid from her back and set off on foot towards the light.

As he drew nearer to it he saw that it was coming from the mouth of a narrow cave in the hill-side, and this puzzled him considerably for there had certainly been no cave there on the other occasions he had visited the pasture. Then he noticed that there was a man standing by the entrance to the cave, and this made him very cautious of approaching it. His walk across the grass grew slower and slower, and a dozen yards from the cave he halted altogether.

The man at the cave-mouth was looking towards him but he did not move or speak, and after some moments of this staring Hob took courage again. Slowly he closed the gap between them till he was only a few feet from the man.

He was young and slender, Hob saw then, and he wore a suit of green under his long flowing cloak. His face was handsome. His fair fell curling down to his shoulders, and as Hob noticed all this he wondered what had brought him to such a lonely place at this late hour. But still he did not venture to speak for he had no idea how to address a stranger with such a rich-looking and elegant appearance.

It was the young man who spoke first. He said, 'Good-evening to you, Hob Hazeldene,' and at the sound of his voice Hob knew instantly that, for all he looked so different from his former self, it was the Ferlie who stood there.

'I – I never meant to come here tonight, Ferlie,' he said uncertainly, and the Ferlie nodded. 'So I thought,' he said, 'and that was why we came to you, instead. There is no mortal who once sees the ferlie riders, but longs to see them again.'

Hob gaped, astonished at the way the Ferlie had read what was in his mind. 'I would fine like another look at them,' he admitted.

'Come with me, then,' the Ferlie told him, 'and you shall see them again.' He pointed to the mouth of the cave. 'Here is the entrance to the ferlie world, Hob.'

'Oh, no!' Hob exclaimed, shrinking back. 'I canna go into your world, Ferlie. I told ye I wouldna go!'

'What d'ye think about when ye play my music, Hob?' the Ferlie asked softly. 'Is there a longing grips ye then – a longing for something ye canna name?'

'Aye,' Hob admitted. 'I do feel like that. I canna tell what it is I want when I play that music – but I want it sorely!'

'You can have it now,' the Ferlie told him. 'It is the ferlie world that calls to you in the music, Hob, and the ferlie world is waiting now to welcome you in. Come with me now, and I promise you that longing will be satisfied.'

'I would never come back if I went in there,' Hob said, shrinking still further away.

'Aye, ye would,' the Ferlie insisted. 'Ye could come out any time ye want, Hob. I'm only asking you to come and have a look. One wee look wouldna harm now, would it?'

'And I could come back any time I wanted?' Hob demanded.

'Och, aye,' the Ferlie said airily. 'Any time!'

Hob felt his resolve weakening at this, as it had weakened when he saw the ferlie host. Also, the handsome young man standing there smiling at him was so different from the strange creature who had tried to trap him before that he did not feel the same sense of danger with him.

He moved cautiously forward. The Ferlie smiled at him again and said encouragingly, 'That's right, Hob. There's nothing to be feared of,' and walked into the cave, beckoning Hob after him.

With a strange mixture of fear and excitement in his heart Hob followed the Ferlie into the cave and found that it continued into a dim, narrow passage which sloped downwards. At the end of this passage was an archway with a bright light of some kind beyond it. The Ferlie stopped at this archway. 'Close your eyes, Hob,' he commanded. Hob closed his eyes and seizing him by the hand the Ferlie pulled him through the archway. 'Now,' he said, 'the ferlie world lies before you. Open your eyes and look at it, Hob!'

Hob opened his eyes, but the light that surrounded him was very strong after the dimness of the passage. He had to close his eyes again and blink till he got used to it, but when he could look steadily at the ferlie world he could hardly believe what he saw.

He was standing, so it seemed to him, in a meadow of rich green grass scattered with primroses and small trees with both fruit and blossom growing on them. The blossom was white and sweet-scented, and the fruit looked like apples made of silver. There was music playing somewhere, and in little groups all over the meadow there were ferlies dancing to it. Other ferlies sat feasting under the blossomed trees, and over everything there was a sky of summer blue with the sun shining brightly down from it.

In astonishment and wonder as he looked at this scene, Hob asked, 'How can it be day with the sun shining brightly when we are in the heart of the hill by night?'

'It can be any time ye want in the ferlie world – night or

day,' the Ferlie told him, smiling. 'It can be any place ye want also, for here it is always the time and place you like best to be in.'

The silvery notes of the ferlie riders' hunting horns sounded as he spoke. Looking towards the sound Hob saw their horses appearing over the meadow's sky-line like the white crest of a wave rising above a green sea, and waited, breathless with excitement, as they came surging towards the place where he stood beside the Ferlie.

In a silent rush of soundless silver hooves they passed him by, and looking up beyond the slim, prancing legs of the horses he saw the graceful forms of the riders, with faces pale as pearl above their cloaks of green silk and silver, collars of gold clasping their slender throats, and circlets of gold set on heads so shining fair that it was hard to tell where the gold of their crowns ended and the gold of their hair began.

Dazzled, he raised a hand to shield his eyes from the sight of such strange, unearthly beauty, and like this he stood watching till the tall white horses had disappeared again over the meadow's further horizon. Then he turned back towards the ferlies enjoying themselves in the sunshine. They were all young, all handsome, and all gay, and as he had longed to see the ferlie riders once more, so he felt that he could never have enough of looking at them and their world of feasting and flowers.

'Ye would never again be cold or hungry or frightened if ye stayed here with us, Hob,' the Ferlie said softly at his elbow. 'Ye would wear fine clothes like us, eat the rich food we eat, and have the same freedom to come and go unseen that we have. Would ye no like that?'

'Aye,' Hob agreed with a sigh. 'I would like it fine.'

'And ye are no wanted in Big Archie's keep,' the Ferlie reminded him. 'So why no stay where ye *are* wanted?'

'Dinna tempt me again, Ferlie,' Hob said. 'Ye ken fine I couldna belong to a world like this.'

'There's part of ye belongs here already,' said the Ferlie, smiling.

Hob looked wonderingly at him. 'What part of me could belong to your world?' he asked.

'You can hear music in the wind, in the voice of the river, in the bees' hum and in singing grasses,' the Ferlie told him. 'Have ye never asked yourself why this should be so, when you lie dreaming in the sun, or where this music comes from?'

'Aye,' Hob admitted. 'Sometimes I have.'

'Then I'll tell ye the answer to your wondering,' the Ferlie said. 'It comes from this world, Hob, for this is a land of dreams. This is the world of perfect beauty and eternal youth that mortals dreamed of and lost so long ago that they have forgotten even the dream of it.'

'But *I* am mortal, Ferlie!' Hob cried. 'Why can I hear it?'

'There are still a few mortals born with the gift of dreams,' the Ferlie said softly. 'You are one of them, and so there is a part of your mind that is in tune with our world the way the notes of a whistle are in tune with one another. It is that part of your mind that can hear the music of our world, and that has given you the power to make an enchanted whistle. And that is the part of you that belongs here.'

'I dinna believe ye, Ferlie,' Hob said, but in spite of this denial he knew that the Ferlie's words had explained a lot that had been a mystery to him before, and he felt in his heart that they were true.

The Ferlie only smiled at his protest. 'It doesna matter what ye believe,' he said. 'Ye canna put that part of yourself away from you, Hob – not till you have decided which world should claim you in the end – your own world or the ferlie world. Sooner or later, you will find, you will have to make that choice, for there will be no peace for you till you do.'

Hob looked down at his feet and then up to the sky, his mind in such a whirl with all this that he did not know what to think, and with his voice now dropped to a coaxing whisper the Ferlie urged him, 'Choose, Hob! Choose now! Will ye be happy here with us, or unhappy in your own world?'

'I'm no sure, Ferlie,' Hob said helplessly. 'I'm just no sure.'

He stared again at the gay scene before him. It should have been a happy sight, he thought, but now there was something about it that chilled him and warned him not to yield to the Ferlie's tempting. It was very hard to make up his mind, all the same, standing there in the sunshine with the soft music playing and the Ferlie's coaxing voice in his ears. He tried to forget the little chill of warning he had felt but he could not put it from his mind, and with a sigh he said at last:

'No, Ferlie. I willna stay here.'

'Now ye're talking foolishly,' the Ferlie told him sharply. 'There is everything here in this world that a mortal could want. Moreover, there is no sickness or sorrow here, and we cannot die, so what more *could* you ask for?'

'One thing,' Hob said, 'but it is the one thing your world doesna have.'

'Name it, then!' the Ferlie cried. 'Name it!'

Hob had to think for a few moments before he could answer this because, although he knew what he wanted to say, he found it hard to put into words. When he found his tongue at last he said slowly:

'If there is no sickness or sorrow or death in your world, Ferlie, then there is no love in it either, for it is when such things strike at people that they are warm and kindly to one another. That is why I dinna want to stay here. I dinna want to stay in a world without love.'

The Ferlie gave a shout of laughter at this. 'There is no love in your world either,' he said spitefully when he had done laughing. 'Not for *you*, anyway, Hob!'

'I ken that,' Hob retorted, stung by the Ferlie's laughter, 'but here there is not even a hope of love, and in my own world there is still hope!'

He turned to go on these words but the Ferlie gave a sudden loud clap of his hands and cried, 'Willing or no, Hob Hazeldene, ye must stay, for you have put yourself in our power by entering here!'

CHAPTER NINE

Hob and Marget

A sudden hush fell on the bright meadow at the sound of the Ferlie's hand-clap. The music stopped playing, and the ferlies who had been feasting and dancing turned to look at Hob. Slowly they began to move towards him and, grinning, the Ferlie said:

'Your good luck has run out, Hob!'

'Ye said I could go back whenever I wanted,' Hob cried. 'Ye promised, Ferlie!'

'The only promise I made,' said the Ferlie, 'was that the longing you felt would be satisfied. And I have kept that promise, for you have only to stay here and you will never feel it again.'

For a moment then, Hob almost panicked. He began to tremble, and clenching his fists he thrust them into his pockets to hide their shaking from the Ferlie. The knuckles of his right hand struck against the shoe Jinty had cast, and suddenly he realized that he still had a way of escape left.

Long ago, he remembered, Goody Cunningham had told him that a horse-shoe was a powerful charm against ferlie magic. '*But only if it is held with the points upwards,*' she had warned. '*If the points of the shoe are turned downwards, all your good luck will run out of them.*'

Hob felt around the shoe with his fingers. It *was* lying with its points turned upwards, and with a flourish he pulled it out of his pocket and held it up between himself and the Ferlie.

'Ye're wrong for the last time, Ferlie!' he shouted. '*Here* is my good luck – and it is no run out yet!'

The Ferlie gave a scream of rage and reached out to grab hold of him, but Hob held the horse-shoe up like a shield in front of him and the Ferlie's hand could not pass it.

Slowly Hob stepped backwards to the arch, still holding the horse-shoe up before himself like a shield. 'Hob!' the Ferlie cried in a pleading voice, and all the other ferlies stretched out their hands to him calling, '*Hob! Hob! Stay with us, Hob!*'

There was a sweet wailing tone to their voices that was like the sound of the ferlie music. Hob trembled again when he heard it for he knew that if he stayed to listen to it the charm of its sound would draw him back into the ferlie world.

He kept backing away, doing his best not to hear the persuading music of their voices, and with every second he held out against them the ferlie world before him grew dimmer and the ferlie voices grew fainter. He gained the arch, and as he took a backward step through it the bright forms of the ferlies faded suddenly to pale ghosts that beckoned to him and called in plaintive whispers. The fading sunshine of their world was swallowed up in darkness, and turning from it Hob ran quickly up the passage and out into the upper world.

The cave at the end of the passage was dark now also, but outside it the moon lay white on the grass and the form of Jinty grazing at the edge of the pasture stood out black against the moonlight. Hob ran to her and swung himself on her back, but as he turned her head for home he was feeling none of the triumph he had expected to feel at escaping from the ferlie world.

It would have been so wonderful in so many ways to have stayed there, he thought, as he rode back towards the keep. He had maybe been foolish in choosing a very uncertain hope in the future instead of the present pleasures the Ferlie had offered him. The sound of the Ferlie's jeering laughter came back into his mind and he remembered him saying, *'There is no love in your world, either – not for you, anyway.'*

He *had* been a fool, Hob told himself, thinking of the old life of hunger and loneliness that lay ahead of him, and he rode home slowly with his chin sunk on his chest and regrets for the vanished world of the ferlies in his mind.

He was so taken up with his thoughts that he was quite close to the keep before he realized that someone holding a lantern was standing by the stable door. At first he thought that Big Archie must somehow have discovered that he had taken Jinty out and was waiting to catch him red-handed. Then he realized that the figure beside the stable was much too small for Big Archie, and when he came into the stable-yard he saw that it was Marget.

He rode Jinty up to her and slid to the ground whispering, 'Marget! What brings ye here? Did Mistress Kate send ye to spy on me?'

'I wouldna spy on ye, Hob!' Marget protested. 'I couldna manage to leave the pantry unlocked for ye tonight, and so I crept downstairs after Mistress Kate was in bed and stole her keys. Then I got some food for ye, but ye werena in the stable-loft when I went up there.'

'Is it you that's been leaving doors unlocked for me to steal food these past three days?' Hob asked in surprise. 'I thought it was just Mistress Kate's carelessness that left them open!'

Marget laughed at this. 'My, but ye're stupid, Hob!' she exclaimed. 'Mistress Kate locks up like a jailer every night – but I ken where she keeps the keys, and so I just unlocked any door I thought would be handy for you.'

'That was good of ye, Marget,' Hob said gratefully. Then he noticed she was shivering although she had a shawl wrapped round her, and he asked, 'Have ye waited here long?'

'Aye,' Marget nodded. 'A long time. I thought ye must have gone to see the Ferlie again when I found the loft empty, and I was feared something had happened to ye. Where *have* ye been, Hob?'

'With the Ferlie,' Hob told her. 'He showed me the ferlie world and wanted me to stay in it, but I told him I didna want to stay.'

'I'm glad ye told him that, Hob,' Marget said. 'I would have missed ye if ye had stayed in the ferlie world.'

This was another surprise for Hob. 'Truly, Marget?' he asked uncertainly. 'Would ye – would ye truly have missed me?'

'Of course I would!' Marget cried. Then, in a voice as uncertain as Hob's own, she added. 'I'm lonely too, Hob.'

'I never thought of that,' Hob told her, blushing to think how selfish he had been.

'Well, ye ken now,' Marget said. 'And – and I'm gey fond of ye, Hob.'

'Well!' said Hob. 'Well, that's just fine, Marget, because I've always been gey fond of you!'

They stood smiling at one another in the dim light of Marget's lantern. 'This food in the basket's cold now,' she told him. 'Put Jinty back in the stable and we'll go quietly up to the kitchen. I have some soup simmering at the side of the fire there.'

She helped Hob to swing open the stable door and he quickly put Jinty back in her stall. Then the two of them went into the keep and crept quietly up the stairs to the kitchen. Marget threw aside her shawl and put some fresh wood on the fire. It was mutton broth she had simmering at the side of it, and when the wood blazed up she ladled out two bowls of this broth, handed one to Hob and took the other for herself.

With their bowls in their laps Marget and Hob sat down in front of the fire, and Marget said, 'Tell me about the ferlie world, Hob. Was it a fine place?'

Hob sniffed the rich smell wafting up from his broth and wriggled his bare toes in the warmth of the fire. Then he looked from the red flames to Marget smiling at him over her bowl, and thought to himself that the Ferlie had been wrong to tell him that there was no love for him in his own world, and that he had made the right choice after all.

'The ferlie world was fine enough,' he told Marget, 'but it was no so fine as this!'

'I'm glad ye think so,' Marget said, smiling. She took a spoonful of her broth and began playing the old game that children play in Scotland with this kind of soup.

'There's peas in it, and beans in it, and leeks in it!' she chanted, looking into the spoon and naming all the vegetables there. Then she downed the lot in a quick swallow.

Hob took his first spoonful, looked to see what was in it and then chanted, 'There's barley in it, and leeks in it, and onions in it, and peas in it, and beans in it!'

He swallowed his soup and Marget chanted over her next spoonful, 'There's tatties in it, and barley in it, and peas in it, and neeps in it!'

Spoonful by spoonful like this, they carried on the contest to see who would be the first to get every kind of vegetable in the broth into one spoonful. It was a good game and one that they never got the chance to laugh over when Mistress Kate was around, but when the broth was finished Marget became serious again.

'It would be fine to get away from this place, would it no, Hob?' she asked.

'Aye,' Hob agreed. 'But where could we go?'

'I heard tell the other day,' Marget said, 'that there's a farmer over Jedburgh way has work for a kitchen-lass and a herd-boy, and they say he is a kind maister.'

She sighed. 'But Big Archie and Mistress Kate would never let us go, of course.'

'We could run away!' Hob said – much to his own surprise for he had never thought of such a thing till that moment.

'We could and all!' Marget exclaimed, as surprised as Hob was himself at the freshness and daring of this idea.

They sat staring at one another as it took hold of their minds, and then Marget asked timidly, 'When would we go, Hob, if we *were* to run away?'

'Now!' Hob said determinedly. 'We'll go this very minute, before anything can happen to stop us.'

'It's a long way to Jedburgh,' Marget reminded him. 'I'll get that basket of food to take with us.'

She jumped up from her seat, then stopped short at a sudden noise from outside the kitchen door. 'What was that?' she whispered.

'I dinna hear anything,' Hob said. They both listened intently, but there was no further sound. 'There's nobody there, Marget,' Hob decided – but in this he was wrong, for Mistress Kate was there!

She was bending down with her ear to the keyhole, for it so happened that she had noticed food had been going missing from her various stores, and that night she had lain awake with the intention of catching the guilty one red-handed. Hob and Marget's laughter over their soup had reached her sharp ears, and she had crept downstairs to listen in to their conversation.

Now, as she heard them coming towards the kitchen door, she dodged quickly up beyond a bend in the stairs, and while they stole quietly down the stairs to the outer door of the keep she stole as quietly upstairs to waken Big Archie.

'Get up! Get up, Big Archie!' she whispered, grabbing him by the shoulder and shaking him hard. 'Hob's running away!'

'Eh? What's that? What's that about Hob?' Big Archie grunted sleepily.

'He's running away and he's got Marget with him,' Mistress Kate hissed. 'Ye've got to get up and stop him!'

'Have ye wakened me to tell me that!' Big Archie demanded crossly. 'Stop him yourself, woman!'

'But he's a warlock,' Mistress Kate cried, 'and I'm feared to meddle with a warlock!'

'Then why d'ye want me to stop him?' Big Archie asked in surprise. 'Ye've said a hundred times ye couldna bide easy with him near ye since he whistled up the ferlie cattle.'

'The Devil fly off with Hob Hazeldene!' Mistress Kate cried out in a rage. 'It's Marget I'm bothered about! She's a good worker, and I say you must stop that Hob taking her away with him.'

Big Archie sat up in bed and scratched his head while he considered what he should do. His conscience was still troubling him over the harm he had done Hob by forcing him to whistle up the ferlie cattle. Also, he was beginning to realize that he had led Hob a pretty poor life on the whole, and that Marget had been no better off with Mistress Kate. He had felt guilty about this from time to time and now, when he thought of Marget and Hob scurrying fearfully away through the dark, he felt even more guilty.

'No,' he decided at last. 'I'll no go after them. They can run away if they like, Kate.'

Mistress Kate opened her mouth to protest but Big Archie gave her no chance to speak, for being wakened in the middle of the night had not done his temper any good. 'Not another word, woman!' he roared in a terrible voice. 'Get back into bed and dinna let me hear another word from ye!'

Mistress Kate glared at him, but she knew of old that there was no use in arguing with Big Archie when he was in this kind of mood. She had to admit she was beaten, and still glaring her rage at him she climbed unwillingly back into bed.

'Now,' said Big Archie, 'lie down and listen to me.'

Mistress Kate lay back sulkily on her pillow. Big Archie lay down also and said, 'Now listen, Kate. Hob and Marget are only bairns, after all, and between us we've led them a poor life. If they think they can find a better one somewhere else, they've a right to seek it. So just forget about chasing after them, and pray the Lord he'll treat you kinder than we treated them.'

'I never wished them any harm,' Mistress Kate snapped.

'Nor did I,' said Big Archie, 'but we're both quick-tempered, Kate, and life with us is no bed of roses.'

'The Lord canna blame me for the quick temper He gave me,' Mistress Kate protested.

'Tell that,' jeered Big Archie, 'to the Lord!'

This gave Mistress Kate so much food for thought that he was asleep again before she could decide on an answer, and so, with a sigh and a conscience that was beginning to feel as heavy as lead, she turned over and tried to go to sleep herself.

Meanwhile, Marget and Hob were making progress down the road. It was dark, for the moon had gone down, and after the first few hundred yards away from the keep Marget began to lag behind a little. Hob looked over his shoulder at her and asked:

'What's wrong, Marget? Are ye feared of walking in the dark?'

'A wee bit,' Marget said uncertainly.

'Ach, that's daft,' Hob told her. 'I'm here to look after ye, am I no?'

'Aye, Hob,' Marget agreed, but still her steps lagged a little and Hob turned to her again. 'Here, I'll take your basket,' he said. Marget handed the basket to him. He slung it on his arm and held out his other hand.

'Come on, Marget,' he said. Marget took his hand and they walked on together with her now quite happily keeping the same pace as himself.

Hob was feeling very cheerful as he walked. A lot of strange things had happened to him since he first made his whistle, he thought, and no doubt people would go on saying that he was a warlock and that it was the Ferlie who had taught him how to make his enchanted whistle. But it was something better than that he had learned from the Ferlie!

If he had never met the Ferlie, he decided, he would never have gone out on Saint John's eve; Marget would not have waited for him, and he would never have learned what it was like to find that there was someone who cared for him!

'Hob,' Marget said after they had gone some distance further, 'I've only heard that wee bit of the ferlie music ye were playing when ye led the white bull into the yard. What like does the whole tune sound?'

'Like this,' said Hob, letting go her hand as he reached for his whistle. He raised the whistle and pursed his lips to the mouth-piece, but for the life of him he could not recall a single note of the ferlie music. And the whistle did not sound like it had before, either. It was only an ordinary whistle now, just like all the others he had made before it. Oddly enough, however, he found that this did not worry him at all, and so he put his whistle back into his pocket and said cheerfully:

'Ach, I forget that tune now, Marget. But never mind. I'll play you other tunes – real bonny ones – when we reach Jedburgh.'

Marget smiled in the darkness at this for, although she knew nothing of Hob's last conversation with the Ferlie, she was wise beyond her years and she knew that he would be happier now with only his own tunes to play than he could ever be with the ferlie music.

'I like your tunes best anyway,' she said, and put her hand in Hob's again.

Marget had a nice warm hand and Hob liked the feeling that he was looking after her. Also, he was enjoying the sense of adventure in their situation, and he thought to himself that they would easily get work in Jedburgh.

'We'll easy get work in Jedburgh, Marget,' he said aloud.

And so they did, and a kind master into the bargain, and that – so far as *they* were concerned anyway – was the best of all possible endings to the story of the Ferlie and the enchanted whistle.

The Kelpie's Pearls

Another exciting and much-loved tale from

MOLLIE HUNTER

Kelpies are water-spirits with magic powers. Of course, no-one believes in such things nowadays, but Torquil did because he had seen one talking to Morag MacLeod. And he believed it was the kelpie who raised the Loch Ness Monster. Certainly some very mysterious things happened that summer. Everyone might have got nearer the truth if only they'd known about the kelpie's pearls.

The Granny Project

ANNE FINE

To the four children, Ivan, Sophie, Tanya and Nicholas, Granny is a bit of a dotty old lady – sometimes demanding, sometimes a nuisance and often annoying – as much a part of their lives as the shambly house or the whirring washing machine. How can Natasha, their eccentric Russian mother, and Henry, their amenable father, decide to put her in a Home?

'Black comedy . . . a whole cast of characters that's totally unique'

Booklist

'Anne Fine writes unsentimentally, credibly and with humour on this tricky subject.'

The Sunday Telegraph

These and other Magnet Books are available at your bookshop or newsagent. In case of difficulties, orders may be sent to:

Magnet Books
Cash Sales Department
PO Box 11
Falmouth
Cornwall TR10 9EN
England

Please send cheque or postal order, no currency, for purchase price quoted and allow the following for postage and packing:

UK
customers

Please allow 45p for first book, plus 20p for the second book and 14p for each additional book ordered, to a maximum charge of £1.63.

BFPO
and Eire

Please allow 45p for the first book, plus 20p for the seond book and 14p per copy for the next 7 books, thereafter 8p per book.

Overseas
customers

Please allow 75p for the first book, plus 21p per copy for each additional book.

While every effort is made to keep prices low, it is sometimes necessary to increase prices at short notice. Magnet Books reserve the right to show new retail prices on covers which may differ from those previously advertised in the text or elsewhere.